Shadows

The Midnight Sun

Also Available from LutheranLibrary.org

- *The Hour Struck* by Dan Patch
- *The Jesuit* by Joseph Hocking
- *The Purple Robe* by Joseph Hocking

◊ *"Map of Norway Under Nazi Domination"*

About The Lutheran Library

The Lutheran Library is a non-profit publisher of good Christian books. All are available in a variety of formats for use by anyone for free or at very little cost. There are never any licensing fees.

We are Bible believing Christians who subscribe wholeheartedly to the Augsburg Confession as an accurate summary of Scripture, the chief article of which is Justification by Faith. Our purpose is to make available solid and encouraging material to strengthen believers in Christ.

Prayers are requested for the next generation, that the Lord will plant in them a love of the truth, such that the hard-learned lessons of the past will not be forgotten.

Please let others know of these books and this completely volunteer endeavor. May God bless you and keep you, help you, defend you, and lead you to know the depths of His kindness and love.

Shadows Under The Midnight Sun

By Ken Anderson

AUTHOR "THE DOCTOR'S RETURN", ETC.

Grand Rapids, Michigan

ZONDERVAN PUBLISHING HOUSE

© 1943 / 2019

LutheranLibrary.org

Copyright Notice

Dedication

Dedicated To
my wife's parents,
Mr. and Mrs. Owen Jones,
with, also, an expression
of gratitude to Mrs. Carl O. Anderson,
a native of Norway,
and her daughter, Eleanor,
for their assistance.

Table of Contents

Also Available from LutheranLibrary.org.............ii

About The Lutheran Library.....................v

Copyright Notice...........................viii

Preface by Lutheran Librarian....................xiii

One...................................I

Two..................................15

Three.................................29

Four.................................41

Five.................................49

Six..................................59

Seven................................65

Eight................................73

Nine.................................83

Ten.................................91

Eleven...............................97

Twelve..............................115

Thirteen.............................129

Fourteen.............................143

Fifteen..............................149

Sixteen..............................163

Seventeen............................175

Eighteen.............................187

Nineteen.............................193

Twenty..............................203

How Can You Find Peace With God?.........207

Benediction...208
More Than 100 Good Christian Books For You To
Download And Enjoy..209

Preface by Lutheran Librarian

In republishing this book, we seek to introduce this author to a new generation of those seeking spiritual truth.

Ken Anderson (1917-2007) wrote more than 70 Christian books for teenagers and adults. He is best known for producing the 1979 film version of John Bunyan's Pilgrim's Progress.

The Lutheran Library Publishing Ministry finds, restores and republishes good, readable books from Lutheran authors and those of other sound Christian traditions. All titles are available at little to no cost in proofread and freshly typeset editions. Many free e-books are available at our website LutheranLibrary.org. Please enjoy this book and let others know about this completely volunteer service to God's people. May the Lord bless you and bring you peace.

One

SECLUDED IN A VALLEY, where a finger of Oslo Fjord penetrated inland, lay the village of Bjerkely—named generations ago by ruddy offspring of the Vikings who loved the great birch woodlands on the rolling *bakke* that dip their feet in the fjord waters. Bjerkely was hidden this night by darkness—thick darkness brooding over the *bakke* summits like a giant wood-grouse keeping warm the eggs of her nest.

But Bjerkely itself was not dark, for a nation that generates twenty per cent more electrical current in proportion to her population than any other country in the world does not ask her people to retire at dusk, nor sit in dimly lighted rooms while the winter sun hides above the Arctic Circle. Bright lights beamed from windoWs of every house, as though happy for the contented families inside where children romped, mothers knitted, fathers read, and old folk relived the years A. that had long since passed out of the cradle of time into the crypt of time.

Nearly every window of the minister's house—sandwiched by the village and *prestegaarden* (church farm) —peered into the night. For lovely Borghild Gran, daughter of Prest Erling Gran, was expecting Bjarne Kolstad, reporter for the Oslo *Morgenbladet* and *Aftenposten*, this evening.

A protective cape was over her shoulders, as, at her dressing table, she increased the glow of her Scandinavian-blond hair by swift strokes of a brush. Rosy cheeks, her only cosmetic, broke into dimples beneath the bright blue eyes peering back from the mirror and suggesting that Bjarne, who could have had the affection of any of many Norwegian girls, would be pleased. When the last curl was in place, she stood, smoothed her Parisian frock, sprayed perfume into her hair, tied her sport oxfords, and descended the stairs—as gracefully as ever the lovely Ingeborg went to meet her gallant Frithjof.

Lars, her pre-adolescent brother—who, with her, had mourned the death of her mother since December of 1938, a month after the death of Queen Maud—was perched on the bottom step.

"Bedtime—" she started to remind him.

"Father has company," Lars whispered.

Smiling down at his red face, Still frosty from an afternoon skiing (he was already old enough to try the dangerous Norwegian ski-sport, slalom) on the fjord, she asked, "Nothing so unusual about that, is there? Has Bjarne—?"

"They look important."

"Important?" She chuckled, "Members of Parliament? Musicians? Or maybe the Bishop?"

"Germans," he informed her, "fish buyers."

"Interesting! I've heard that the catches are large this year, especially large around the Lofotens."

"Then," Lars pleaded, "may I stay up and listen? They tell interesting stories, and—and—sometimes the fish buyers give candy and gum to children. The buyers are giving away lots of gum and candy this year."

"They perhaps want good prices. The war has made quite a demand in Germany."

"May I stay up?" Lars asked.

"Until the clock strikes ten, dear. Is that fair enough?"

He nodded.

Borghild hesitated in the hall a moment. Bjarne was always on time, and so when the door chimes sounded she was not surprised.

Lars could have watched the scene, but politely (or was it for the bribe of the new skis—good enough to Win the Birkebeiner ski race!—Bjarne had brought. last time he was home?) gave ears and eyes to the parlor, where his father was entertaining his guests.

"We are getting good fish from the Norwegians," Bruno Schreckenbach, spokesman of the group of three German nationals, said. "War conditions in the beloved fatherland have greatly increased the demand. We are fortunate to have your people for our friends!"

"Our largest need is cod," another said. "The people whom we conquer—that is, protect temporarily—are pitifully undernourished. Even the soldiers! Poor management! Poor government! The liver oil helps our social workers and our doctors in their humanitarian interests."

As though he had taken a cue, Schreckenbach added, "The people we have delivered from British domination are given every opportunity to approach as nearly as possible the physical superiority of our master race!"

Prest Erling Gran stared at replicas of Backer's *Opdal Church* and Balke's *Lighthouse* on the opposite wall. The Church! The Light! His quests! His life! Perhaps that was why his face, though usually quick to smile, was a little stern.

Leif Hunseid, Bjerkely merchant, mayor and hotel owner, whose mother had been a native of Germany and Whose father was half German, broke the brief silence, saying, "Employees from the German Consulate in Oslo were in my store today and bought skis. They're spending the week here, they said—a late Winter vacation."

"But we can't expect the Germans to equal the Norwegians in skiing," Schreckenbach laughed. "I visited the ski museum at Frognerseteren last time I was in Norway. I believe they had a ski there dated 2,500 B.C."

One of his partners chuckled, "I took one look at Huseby Hill, when I motored out of Oslo the other day, and decided to limit my skiing to slight inclines."

"Our people love to ski," Prest Gran said simply.

Across the room from Schreckenbach was Fearnley's masterpiece, LabrofossenF—where the artist's brush has formed a broad and foaming cascade; a nude pine with its dead trunk pointing to wet clouds overhead; the dark forest in the background; derelict logs in an eddy's snare, with an eagle, the only living thing in this sublime waste, perched upon them. Studying the painting, he said, "Norway is a great country, and Germany is proud to have her for a friend! As long as there is a Germany, this beauty shall be free!"

"You are not going to occupy Norway?" the minister asked quickly.

"Of course not!" Bruno Schreckenbach managed a laugh. Then, with a flourish,of words that suggested plagiarism from the works of a mustached Austrian orator, he stormed, "But the invincible forces of the Nazi State will exterminate any swine who attempts to molest our beloved friends, the Scandinavians! It is less than three weeks ago since a British submarine sunk a German freighter in the Skagerrak! It may not be three more weeks until we shall have put an end to these—these sneak thieves of the coward Henderson! But Norway? Our eternal friends!"

Borghild's laughter came from the hall.

"I would like for you to meet my daughter," Prest Gran interrupted, "and her fiancé—a reporter for the Morgenbladet and the Aftenposten. He's well informed on current events."

Behind his back the minister did not see how pleased the men were at the mention of a news reporter.

"But, Father," Borghild was protesting, as the three Norwegians entered, "we don't want to interrupt your —"

Bjarne injected, "We were going for a walk anyway. We—"

"Nonsense!" Prest Gran laughed. "These men are at their leisure. I couldn't sell them more than our six goldfish, you know. Or didn't Birgit say that one of the fish died yesterday? Leif Hunseid brought them for a visit."

The strangers stood and were individually introduced. Then they sat down again. But Schreckenbach was the last to return to his chair, for his eyes feasted on Borghild's beauty. Every grace and beauty of the Norwegian girl seemed to be found in her, and he was stunned.

He did not see Bjarne's scowl. But Borghild did, and she said, "Oh, I forgot. Will you excuse me, please? You men will have more in common." Without waiting for permission, she left the room, taking Bruno Schreckenbach's eyes with her until she disappeared, only to remain in the room on the throne of his memory.

But Schreckenbach could not let a woman waste, opportunity, as, cautiously, he said to Bjarne, "You are a reporter, Prest Gran tells me."

Trying to be cordial, Bjarne smiled, "That's right. How about an interview?"

"The typical reporter!" one of the buyers laughed. "They're all the same—from Tromso to Cape Town."

"Always on the alert for a scoop," Bjarne said.

"Well," Schreckenbach ventured, "what do you think of the war?"

"The *phony war*, as they call it? You folk say blitzkrieg, but I understand the English-speaking people have another word for it—*sitzkrieg*, they call it."

Schreckenbach's face grew crimson, either from embarrassment or else from anger.

Bjarne replied, "Well, it makes good business for the newspapers. Big news, when German planes were seen reconnoitering over Oslo, Bergen and Kristiansand a week ago Saturday."

"You know why, don't you?" Schreckenbach snapped.- "If some day R. A. F. planes should land in your—"

"But," Bjarne scoffed noticeably, "you don't think that's possible, do you?"

"You don't think it is secret any longer that the British have been negotiating with your government since the first of the year?" Schreckenbach asked. "And why? So she can occupy you with her soldiers."

"But not without permission," Bjarne reminded. "We were neutral during the last war, at great loss to our merchant marines, and we'll be neutral this time, too. I can honestly say, as a newsman, that since your invasion of Poland last September, there hasn't been the slightest Norwegian inclination expressed as to participation. If we have our choice, we shall be neutral."

"The Reich will never disturb your neutrality. A year ago, when I heard our beloved Fuehrer, Adolph Hitler, address the Reichstag, he said that no Scandinavian statesmen could contend that Germany had ever put a request of any nature to them which would suggest transgression of the sovereignty and integrity of your state."

"But," Bjarne's eye, bold above sinewy shoulders and thick jaws, winked, "a promise of that nature was also given Poland, wasn't it?"

"And it was kept, until Poland endangered German interests in Danzig and other sectors!"

"Anyway," Bjarne sighed, "we expect to stay neutral."

"But you have heard news of British mine-laying in Norwegian neutral waters?"

"And we discredit it, of course."

"Discredit it?"

Bjarne chuckled, "Your navy's feud with the British fleet is amusing. We get reports almost daily in the newsroom about German ore freighters leaving Narvik and staying Within the neutral three-mile limit, with British ships watching them like patient cats, until. they reach the comparative safety of the Skagerrak for a mad dash home behind Denmark. And When it was news, we ran a story about the German ship captains staying at Narvik's Grand Hotel, while the British stayed at the Royale. But as far as any fantastic stories about mine-laying, or—"

Schreckenbach became violent, "You Norwegians are too casual about things! Some day the British will invade you! They will rob you of your freedom! They will stain your beautiful country with your own blood! Then you will awaken! And then it will be too late!"

"Gentlemen!" Prest Gran interrupted. "As long as it was a forum, your conversation was interesting, but now that it has become a fray—"

"Sorry," Schreckenbach bowed. "It was only a debate—really." To Bjarne, he smiled and said, "My apologies, please."

"That's quite all right. I'm sorry—"

"Pardon," there was an intruder, "Prest Gran, but we've got the nicest little heifer in the barn you ever saw."

"Good! That's fine, Sigurd! That's splendid!" Prest Gran then proceeded to introduce the newcomer, "Gentlemen, I would like for you to meet Sigurd, my faithful dreng... farmhand, I guess you Germans would call him. But he's more than just an employee. Sometimes," the minister's kind eyes twinkled slyly, "I like so think of him as the foreman around here."

Sigurd Lykke grinned his reply, not a sheepish or an embarrassed grin, but the self-confident grin of one who is as calm in the presence of a prince as in the home of a peasant. He was not young any more, so far as his body was concerned, but age had not taken the zest for pranks and puns out of his nature.

He was a staunch bachelor—for so the girls had ordained!

"Friends of the King or friends of Quisling?" he asked boldly.

Bjarne twinkled with delight; Schreckenbach and his men shrunk a bit.

"Ah," Schreckenbach fumbled for words, "Norway hasn't taken to Mr. Quisling, the Nazi sympathizer, has it?"

"Ho!" Sigurd delighted. "When he tried to start his Nazi Party back in '33 and dressed up his youngsters in brown shirts with swastikas on the arms, we passed a law forbidding anybody but the police and soldiers of the army and navy to wear uniforms. His *Nasjonal Samling* is about as popular as a synagogue in Berlin. And last election his party didn't get enough votes to make an adding machine work up a sweat. We've got a warm spot for Germany, we Norwegians, but we don't cater to you Nazis."

Loquacious Schreckenbach had met his rival, and he was as void of words as a desert is of dew.

"And that paper he publishes," Sigurd continued, "*Fritt Folk*, he calls it. It started out as a daily, but that kind of thing can't get the backing of real Norwegians, and it's only a weekly now—and a poor one at that. Bjarne knows about it. He works in Oslo, too."

"Sigurd," Prest Gran spoke, "ask Birgit if she will serve a lunch."

"Sorry," Schreckenbach burst in, "but we can't take the time. We've got to hurry back to our hotel."

"We," one of the buyers added, "have invoices to go over."

And the third added hastily, "There are so many individual fishermen, and we try to treat each of them fairly."

"But—" the minister began.

"Very kind of you." Bruno Schreckenbach spoke again. "Your typical Norwegian hospitality is tempting, but we must go."

"If you must," Prest Gran conceded. Then he called, "Borghild."

"Yes, Father," as she returned to the room.

"Birgit took these men's wraps. Will you get them?"

"Yes."

Again, Schreckenbach's eyes gave all attention to Borghild's loveliness, and when she gave him his heavy topcoat, he said, "Heavy for you, isn't it?"

She did not answer, as she served the other three visitors likewise.

"Goodbye," Schreckenbach said at the door. "It has been so good to meet you, Prest Gran, and Mr. Kolstad, and Mr. Lykke, and—your lovely daughter."

"Can you find your way back to the first street light?" the minister asked.

"I have a flashlight, if we need it."

They left.

But the flashlight was not used, nor did the men return to the village. Instead, like disciples of the darkness, they crept toward that part of Oslo Fjord which was a mile away.

Inside, Bjarne said, "I hope they weren't offended. It gets tiresome, weeding the truth out of Nazi propaganda day after day. I want those fellows to know that we haven't swallowed the hook anyway."

"Nothing serious," Prest Gran assured. "I only pray that our friendship with Germany won't be altered by the rise of Nazism." Then his eyes teased as he said, "I hardly need to be pardoned to go to my study. It's been two weeks since you were home, hasn't it, Bjarne?"

"Seems like two years," he answered.

"Two decades!" Borghild emphasized.

The parent laughed. "They say time flies for everyone, but for separated lovers it flies on wounded wings." He left them.

"Lars," Borghild whispered, "the clock is striking."

In another moment, she and Bjarne were alone.

"Sweetheart," he said, taking her warm hands in his, "it's good to be here again."

"If Bjerkely weren't so wonderful, I'd want Father to try and be transferred to Oslo, so we could be together. But," she smiled up at him, "we won't always be separated, will we?"

"Never—after our wedding in June. I'm even going to take you to work with me. You can follow me on all my beats, and when I return to the office to get out my copy, I'll set you right up beside my typewriter—sort of for inspiration."

She laughed, "That wouldn't work. Instead of writing, 'There was an automobile accident near Our Saviour's Church,' you'd write, 'Those aesthetic nature lovers, who wander about the edifice like carefree children of Frey, were swept through the gamut from romance to reality by the ugly discord of two automobiles—' Anyway, that wouldn't be the right kind of inspiration, and you might get fired." She shook her finger at him.

He kissed her.

"It isn't cold," she suggested, "and even though it isn't moonlight, we could stroll to the fjord."

"It wouldn't be a visit, would it, without a walk to the fjord?"

"I'll get my wraps."

Outside, they walked briskly until, warmed by exertion, their pace slackened automatically.

"My but it's dark," Borghild said. "Even after one's eyes are accustomed to leaving the light, it's difficult to see. If it weren't for the snow, we'd lose our way."

"Maybe a storm is coming."

"I didn't hear the weather forecast today. It must not be one of those early spring blizzards, though, or we'd have been warned."

"No more blizzards," he said, squeezing her gloved hand. "I would have been back two times last month, you know, but both times there was too much snow for transportation. I interviewed a member of the American Legation at Kjeller Airfield yesterday, and they were just hauling away the last snow from around the runways."

After a moment of silence, except for the rhythm of crunching snow beneath their feet, he continued, "I killed two birds with one stone at the airport. A planeload of government attachés arrived unexpectedly from Berlin, so I sort of scooped the story. The Nazis seem worried at the possibility of Britain's taking possession of the Scandinavian countries. Maybe—" He hesitated, as though he had not intended to say what was almost uttered.

"What?"

"Maybe there'll be fur flying yet."

"Do you think so, Bjarne?"

"I hope not. But—"

"There's no chance of that, is there?"

"I don't know," he told her. "A strange report came into the newsroom yesterday."

"What?"

"On Friday officials of the Norwegian Foreign Office in Berlin were given invitations to see what was called a peace film by German propagandists. And," he dug his toe into the snow, like a warrior making his footing sure while he waits his opponent's first move, "according to the report, the pictures shown to them were terrifying shots of the inhuman bombing of Warsaw."

"How horrible! What was the motive in that?"

"Peace propaganda, the Nazis called it."

"But," Borghild said, "I wouldn't call that peace propaganda."

"That's what one of our men told the German Minister, and the German Minister explained that they were peace propaganda pictures because they warned all observers of what happened to any country which resisted Nazi attempts to defend it from England."

"Ooooh!"

"Probably nothing but an outburst of Nazi fanaticism," Bjarne said. "If the Germans had any intentions of invading us, we'd be getting a lot of ultimatums, like Poland got, and there would be ridiculous reports circulating through the world that Norway was mistreating the Quisling bunch and harming Hitler's regime."

Lifting her face upward, so that her profile, a shade darker than the night, was outlined in detail, Borghild said, "It's so good to know that God knows all about it! He'll take care of us! Why should we worry—ever so little?"

"The Nazis want little to do with God," he said. To which she added, "But God is going to have a lot to do with them one of these days."

They walked on, until the dim outline of Oslo Fjord lay beneath them.

"It's so beautiful," she said, "even in the dark."

She began to hum the national anthem, *Ja vi elsker* ("Yes, we love our country"). And as she hummed, both of them thought of the anthem's lyrics—descriptions of their native land, the wars and events which formed their country and now held it together.

Then, presently, she was singing a hymn she had known since childhood:

> A mighty fortress is our God,
> A bulwark neVer failing;
> Our Helper He, amid the flood
> Of mortal ills prevailing.
> For still our ancient foe
> Doth seek to work us woe;
> His craft and power are great,
> And armed with cruel hate,
> On earth is not his equal.
>
> Did we in our own strength confide,
> Our striving would be losing;
> Were not the right Man on our side,
> The Man of God's own choosing.
> Dost ask who that may be?
> Christ Jesus, it is He;
> Lord Sabaoth His—

"Listen!" Bjarne pulled Borghild with him behind a bush,

whispering as he did, "I'm sure I heard Schreckenbach!"

"Schreckenbach?"

There was no mistaking it when figures came through the darkness, and one German said, "I tell you, I heard singing," in his native tongue, which Bjarne and Borghild both understood.

"So did I!" Schreckenbach cursed. "Some kids on their way home from skiing!"

"But it's dark to ski."

"Dumb swine! Some sentimental boy and girl courting then!" Schreckenbach peered out over the fjord, and whispered in delighted tones, "They should be coming soon!"

"It wouldn't surprise me if the British have submarines in Oslo harbor waiting to—"

"Swine!" Bruno Schreckenbach raged. "Cowardly swine! You doubt the wisdom of the Nazi plans?"

"No, Bruno, but—but if we should fail—if—"

"Fail? When Grand Admiral Erich Raeder carries out his plans, all the navies of the world couldn't stop him! I met Raeder," he whined proudly, "when he began the Model Construction Competition of the Naval League of German Women. Hundreds of German sons joined the navy because of that wise propaganda. And a relative of mine graduated from Miirwik with him. Maybe Kaiser Wilhelm did tell the King of England that 'Germans are landlubbers—afraid of water,' but that was a war ago, before the days of Raeder the raider! If the—"

"Bruno! Listen!"

"Ships! Our fleet! Heil Hitler!"

"Swine!" Schreckenbach snapped. "Signal! Quick!"

As though frozen upright where they stood, Borghild and Bjarne rationed their breaths as they watched the Nazi Trojan horses flash messages to the approaching boats. Then they saw, coming up the fjord, the invasion fleet—an armada of blacked-out fighting vessels creeping, like a twentieth century Black Douglas, to stab a slumbering victim in the back.

There was a faint return signal from the leading ship.

"They saw us!" Schreckenbach rejoiced. "They saw us! Heil Hitler! Hurry now! Back to town! We've got work to do!"

Eagerly the figures disappeared, running, into the darkness in the opposite direction from which they had come.

"B-Bjame," Borghild stammered.

"Come! We've got to get the warning into Oslo! The Nazis are attacking us!"

Two

APRIL 9, 1940, dawned upon Bjerkely while the darkness yet brooded over the flanking *bakke* and the whispering fjord—for the town square was a confusion of people hours before the armies of day invaded the east. After midnight, when, receiving Bjarne's report of Raeder's fleet, the government at Oslo ordered all coast towns blacked out, everyone was soon up, eager to learn of developments.

Bjarne had tried to telephone his newspaper, but after one o'clock, he had given up, saying, "This is an invasion! The telephone operators have a German accent! That's why I don't get my paper!"

And so he gave attention to the radio, looking up at intervals to say, "Colonel Sundlo has turned Narvik over to the Nazis!" or, "The forts of Oscarsborg, Rauö, and Haaöen have been shelled!" or, still more distressing, "The German Air Force is blanketing our ports!"

Prest Gran paced about his house—when he was not at the door giving consolation to some fearful saint or frantic sinner—stooped, as though he bore all of Norway on his shoulders.

Borghild alternated between going to the door, pacing with her father, and standing beside Bjarne.

"It can't be true!" The minister wrung his hands. "It can't be true! Germany has always been our friend! Always! Kaiser Wilhelm himself was vacationing in Sagnefjord when the last war broke out! Germany has been our friend! Our friend!"

The door chimes sounded again.

It was Leif Hunseid who met Borghild at the door, as, through the window, she saw the first glow of dawn.

"Leif Hunseid! Isn't everything horrible?"

"I've sat at my radio until it's driving me mad! I can't wait until morning, so we can do something!"

As she walked beside him to the parlor, she asked, "But what is there we can do?"

"Kolstad," the mayor addressed Bjarne, "can you stand it to listen to the radio?"

"Want to get all I can," Bjarne said, barely looking up, "before even the radio announcers start having Quisling accents! I tried to call my paper—"

"Yes, I know," Hunseid intercepted, "because I've tried to get Oslo, too. My radio suggests that Quisling, and a well-organized force of dirty fifth columnists (to use Franco's term) have taken over! I tell you, it makes me—"

Prest Gran appeared, quite calm now. "Mr. Hunseid," he said.

"Prest Gran! What shall we do?"

"It is difficult to know."

"But," the mayor wrung his hands, "the people in the square demand me to give them counsel! I don't dare to organize anything, until we know what the government wants the people to —"

"Where's Schreckenbach?" Bjarne broke in. "And his henchmen?"

"I don't know," Leif Hunseid answered. "They were staying at my hotel, but after we returned there—after our visit with you here —they excused themselves. I thought they went to their rooms, but —"

"But they went to the fjord!" Bjarne completed. "We should have known something treacherous like this was up, with all of these fish traders and consul—. By the way, Mr. Hunseid, what happened to those consuls who came down from Oslo to ski?"

"Gone—just like Schreckenbach."

"Funny," Bjarne mumbled.

"All things work together for good to them that love God," came from the man of God's lips.

"But we've been stabbed in the back, Prest! We—"

"God knows all about it, Leif. He—"

Leif Hunseid, allergic to anything spiritual, broke in, "Do you suppose it might be well to call a meeting of the townspeople, Prest Gran?"

"A meeting?"

"In the church. You could talk to them, cheer them, and—"

"Say," Bjarne interrupted, "that's a good idea. Norwegians are intelligent, but not immune to mob psychology." Addressing his prospective father-in-law, he continued, "I'd say that's the thing to do!"

Hunseid's face became suddenly radiant.

"That does sound good," Borghild put in.

At this moment, there was a rustling in the kitchen.

"That you, Sigurd?" the minister called.

An affirmative mumble came from the kitchen, followed soon by the appearance of the faithful *dreng*, who carried a hunting rifle which he grasped tensely. "I'm going to shoot the first Nazi I see!"

"But—"

"State of war, isn't it?"

"Put down your gun," Hunseid snapped. "We've got to go at this the right way."

"The right way to kill skunks," Sigurd argued. sans the usual grin, "is to shoot on sight—not go up, and pick 'em up by the tail, and—"

"Mr. Hunseid is right, Sigurd," Prest Gran said. "He'll call a meeting of the townspeople—at the church. We'll try to get organized so we'll be ready to serve the government as soon as orders come."

"That's right," Bjarne put in.

"Yes, Sigurd," from Borghild.

Slowly lowering his gun, Sigurd muttered, "Maybe so."

"We're going to contest this with our lives," Hunseid said, "so if you want that kind of action, it'll come soon enough. But we must go at things intelligently. And, for that matter, all of the Nazis are gone, and—"

"Probably," Sigurd fumed, grasping his gun again, "hiding along the fjord somewhere, just waiting for me to put the bead on them!"

"Possibly, but if you did destroy them, many more would take their places," the mayor continued. "Why don't you go to the square and pass the word around that we'll have a meeting in the church this morning— that's the largest auditorium space available —say," looking at the clock, which was about to strike, "in another hour?"

"All right," Sigurd said, turning to go.

"And leave your gun here," Hunseid urged, "or they'll think you're a Quisling man, too."

"Me?" Sigurd snapped. "I'm a Quislinger like Hitler's a rabbi! I'll go. Here," handing Bjarne his gun, he said, "take this," and left.

"I'll go and have the janitor open the church," Hunseid said, turning to leave. "You'll all be over in an hour?"

"All," Prest Gran answered, "except perhaps Birgit, and Lars, who is asleep."

"Good! I'll see you then. You'll have something for the people?"

The minister nodded, as the mayor left, and hurried to the sanctuary of his study.

"Bjarne!" Borghild trembled, grasping Bjarne's arm, "It's so horrible!"

He was silent.

"Stabbed in the back! The Nazis know we aren't a military nation! Oh, Bjarne, do you think we'll be treated... like... like... Oh, Bjarne!... like the Poles... and the Jews?"

He remained silent, watching the dawn as though he did not know but what it was sunset and this was the end of a doomed man's last day.

"The British will help us, won't they," Borghild asked, "if they can?"

"They can't do much against organized treachery like this," he spoke at last. "There's as much difference between Hitler and

Chamberlain as there is between— between King Haakon and Quisling."

"Perhaps," Borghild ventured, "Prime Minister Chamberlain's peace tactics have been a detriment."

After a long silence, Bjarne said, "His plans were right—but they didn't work. Maybe Winston Churchill will take over now. There seemed to be those in our newsroom who thought he soon would anyway."

"Only a year ago," Borghild added, "Norway awarded the Nobel Peace Prize to Mr. Chamberlain—"

"While Hitler laughed," Bjarne broke in, "and changed from fake tanks, built on automobiles to the real thing—built up his navy—the *Luftwaffe*, and—P" He stopped abruptly to say, "We saw all that, but who ever thought he'd attack us?"

"But the British will help us, won't they? Chamberlain will try to help, won't he?"

"Yes," Bjarne sighed, "of course."

"And," she hesitated, "maybe if Churchill gets in—"

"Even if he's the ancestor of England's greatest general, the Duke of Marlborough, sweetheart, Churchill or nobody else will be able to help us unless something's done soon. The Nazis have been planning this for years! It'll take more than a few weeks of strategy by the Allies to break those plans!"

"But God is on our side," she said.

They went to the radio again, listened to the Troms6 station for the next half hour.

When music followed a news broadcast, Borghild, looking up at the clock, reminded, "Time to go to the church, isn't it?"

Through the window Bjarne saw that a steady stream of people was entering the edifice. He pointed, but did not speak.

"Dear people! So typical of all true Norwegians!"

"Yes," he said, standing. "Get your wraps."

"I will. First, though, I'll tell Birgit to stay home, so we won't need to awaken Lars. Dear boy, he'll find out soon enough!" '

"Good idea," he told her. "They don't need to go."

In a moment, they left the house.

The church was half filled when they entered it, and in another ten minutes all of Bjerkely's men, and many of its women and children, had been packed inside the

sacred walls. Venerable old men, and their yet fair wives, who had been natives of Bjerkely since long before Norway and Sweden became separate, after having been merged decades before by Frederick VI of Denmark in the Treaty of Kiel; the middle-aged who remembered King Edward VII of England's intervention in affairs, when proud King Oscar II of Sweden refused to permit a member of the. Bernadotte family to accept the Norwegian crown; and the newly-married, shocked from their marital bliss by the blustery events, made up the crowd. All were sober—some grimly defiant.

There were whispered undertones, threats, shrill sounds of fear, an occasional tone of optimism.

But all was silent when Leif Hunseid stepped to the front of the communion railing, stared a moment at the ceiling before lowering his eyes to the people.

"People of Bjerkely," he began, fidgeting, "natives of a nation that has challenged the world with its quests for' peace, and right relations with all men... my tongue is bound... I," he bowed his head, bringing tears to ruddy eyes in the pews, eyes that had met subzero blasts without flinching, "I still feel that we'll awaken to find this only a dream... I mean, I wish I could feel that way. But this is real, and it's our duty, as mutual servants of our great King Haakon, to be alert for duty. That is why we are assembled.

"Three fish buyers—or so they said they were—came to the hotel yesterday, and to my office... Germans, they were... and they were very friendly. I was delighted, for, as you all know, my mother was a native of Germany, and I had always been proud of that splendid blood stream. I was schooled there for five years. In

fact, one of the men and I... Schreckenbach was his name... had been classmates, and so our meeting seemed all the more pleasant. ,

"I showed them our town," he said, straining his face, as though to fight tears, "and they were unusually interested... though I, like a blind fool, didn't suspect their treachery. They even wanted to meet Prest Gran, and so we spent some of the evening there.

"But they were not friends," he continued, after a pause, "they were enemies—members of that hideous, Nazi monster pledged to rid the world of all that is worth while and replace it with totalitarian barbarism, like," his voice grew to a tempest, "taking fib'degrb't from the table (after the good things we have had in the past years) and replacing it with garbage!

"You have all heard the news," he continued, "and I need not repeat. It may not be long until attempts will 'be made to occupy every Norwegian town. The employees of the German Consulate in Oslo, who came here to ski, mysteriously had disappeared from the hotel, along with the fish buyers, when news broke out. Where they are hiding, I don't know, but we may well expect that they are planning our fate.

"But we will meet them! We will drown them in our blood, if need be! Bjerkely—as a true blood count of all Norway—shall always be free, even if she must fight to be at peace!"

The church, a sacred place—especially to those Whose spiritual experience had ascended from mere liturgy to vital life in Christ during the spiritual revival which had been sweeping the country—gave resonance to a bursting cheer that would have muted-the strongest-

chord of the organ. I

"Before we dismiss, I shall give you plans for organized resistance (as well as listening to suggestions from you), in the event our town should be threatened. But first, we shall hear from one whose counsels make mine as a child beside a sage... our minister," he bowed, "Prest Gran."

Slowly, Prest Erling Gran ascended his pulpit—for to him clerical attire was not indispensable to delivering a message to the souls he bountifully fed. Before speaking, he bowed his head briefly. When he lifted his face, his hands were seen turning the leaves of the pulpit Bible.

The building was barren of noise, so silent that it seemed the very walls would crash inward from lack of support, as though sucked into a vacuum.

Into this silence came the fatherly voice, reading from the Book:

He that dwelleth in the secret place of the Most High shall abide under the shadow of the Almighty.

I will say of the Lord, He is my refuge and my fortress: my God; in him will I trust.

Surely he shall deliver thee from the snare of the fowler, and from the noisome pestilence.

He shall cover thee with his feathers, and under his wings shalt thou trust: his truth shall be thy shield and buckler. Thou shalt not be afraid for the terror by night; nor for the arrow that flieth by day;

Nor for the pestilence that walketh in darkness; nor for the destruction that wasteth at noonday.

A thousand shall fall at thy side, and ten thousand at thy right hand; but it shall not come nigh thee.

Only with thine eyes shalt thou behold and see the reward of the wicked.

Because thou hast made the Lord, which is my refuge, even the Most High, thy habitation;

There shall no evil befall thee, neither shall any plague come nigh thy dwelling.

For he shall give his angels charge over thee, to keep thee in all thy ways.

Then he looked up from the Book and faced his people.

"I believe," he began, "that these words are spoken to the soul. The Old Testament saint saw God's blessing in tangible things, for he had not learned the full ways of faith. To him God's blessing was manifested in visible things. But there was one among those saints... Job was his name... whose blessings were of the soul, and that is best. Let us seek those graces of God which, though our bodies may be submitted to suffering, will keep our souls in perfect peace.

"Here is real safety, a safety that is not a guarantee upon those transient things we all must leave behind some day, but a sure lock upon the soul that trusts in Christ and His atoning blood. If you have not found this secret place of the Most High, I have no promises for you. But if you have," he smiled, "then you have found a sure fortress; you shall be delivered from this evil which is upon us; you shall be covered with wings of protection—even if the violent forces bearing upon us take from you all that is dear of earthly goods.

"Let us be willing to suffer for His sake—He who suffered as none has ever sufiered, for us! Let us be as willing to suffer for Him as we are to give our lives for

our beloved Norway! If you are one of those lost sheep whom the Master seeks, turn to Him in this hour of dark trial. He shall give light! His truth shall be thy shield and buckler. EVen the jaws of death cannot defeat you then!"

While he spoke, the church organizt had gone to the organ and was playing softly:

Rock of Ages, cleft for me,

Let me hide myself in Thee;

Let the water and the blood, From Thy riven side which flowed, Be of sin the double cure,

Save me from its guilt and pow'r. Not the labors of my hands

Can fulfill Thy law's demands; Could my zeal no respite know, Could my tears forever flow,

All for sin could not atone;

Thou must save, and Thou alone. Nothing in my hand I bring, Simply to Thy Cross I cling; Naked, come to Thee for dress, Helpless, look to Thee for grace; Foul, I to the fountain fly,

Wash me, Saviour, or I die!

"Are you on that rock?" the minister pleaded. "Have you been washed in that fountain? Pray the prayer of the publican this morning, God be merciful to me a sinner, and learn the peace the saints may have in the wake of trouble! Do not—"

The rear door burst open, and Bruno Schreckenbach, in Gestapo uniform, accompanied by the two who had been at Prest Gran's house, entered.

Raising his hand in the Nazi salute, Schreckenbach shouted, "Heil Hitler!"

The eyes of the man at the door and the man in the pulpit locked, like dueling arrows that had struck each other in midair. And the eyes in the pew turned, first toward the .door, then toward the pulpit. The tenseness was like that in the Court of St. James, before the outbreak of hostilities, when Joachim von Ribbentrop, then Germany's ambassador to London, transgressed the rigid etiquette of George VI's first court; instead of bowing to His Majesty, he had thrust his arm into the air three times, and had barked three times, "Heil Hitler!" Then he seized the king's hand and pumped it idiotically. Even the German Foreign Office had called the atrocity a grosse Dummheit, while the British sense of humor rechristened Hitler's envoy, "Brickendrop."

"There is sure refuge in Christ," Prest Gran continued bravely. "Whatever the strength of the adversary, the omnipotent Lamb of God—"

"Heil Hitler!" Schreckenbach saluted again, then bellowed, "Silence in the name of the Gestapo!"

"You have no right—" Prest Gran objected.

"Silence! I come at the command of the great Reich! Heil Hitler!"

' "But—H

"Listen, you fools!" Leif Hunseid stood to object. "You can't come into—"

"Silence!"

There was a foreboding movement among the men in the pews, and, promptly, two machine guns were held in position by Schreckenbach's aides.

Quickly the Gestapo leader goose-stepped to the front of the auditorium.

l

"While you have met," he said, "my men, tourists from the German Consulate, have placed Bjerkely under martial law! Every house is being searched for firearms! You are powerless to resist! No one may leave this building until permission is given! Machine guns guard each exit!"

He smiled now, and the arrogant pride left his face somewhat, as he said, "Believe me, it hurts me to do this. It hurts my beloved Leader to demand it. Every shot fired from a vessel of our invasion fleet, every bomb dropped by the *Luftwaffe*, has found its target only after being aimed by a tear-dimmed eye. You are our friends! Germany loves you! But we cannot permit the British swine to use you as an easy means of hindering the great Nazi program from hurriedly bringing real peace, real justice, real brotherhood to Europe... by purging it of those vile elements that selfishly seek to thwart our noble purpose! Believe me! I am your friend! My men are your friends! Our soldiers are your friends! Our seamen are your friends! Our airmen are your friends! Germany is your friend! Let us work together, so that this friendship need not be broken!"

Saluting, he once more cried, "Heil Hitler," and, with his two henchmen, left the building.

Like an effigy of himself, Prest Gran leaned, motionless, against his pulpit. He did not look up until one of the younger men had shouted, "They can't do this!" and proceeded to the door.

"What are you going to do?" somebody asked him.

"Go outside!" he fumed, as his thumb snapped the latch.

And then there was the sickening splatter of machine-gun bullets against the outside wall, the wail of women, the gasps of men.

"He's been shot!" somebody shouted.

But the young man, his crimson rage turned to pale fear, returned.

"Did they miss?"

"J -Just a warning," he managed to say, "shot above me."

All was very silent now.

Prest Gran descended the pulpit steps and went to the unoccupied front pew of the auditorium, where he poured his tears into the basin of his hands.

"Lars!" Borghild whispered, grasping Bjarne's pulsating arm. "He's home with Birgit!"

"He'll be all right," Bjarne tried to assure.

"But they're searching all the houses! They might hurt him! They're like beasts! They—"

"God will take care of him," he said, caressing her tenderly with his eyes.

And she was comforted.

"What shall we do, Prest?" Leif Hunseid pleaded.

"Have faith in God! Faith is of little use to us, if we don't let the Lord test it and prove it! Haven't you faith?"

Leif Hunseid turned away so no one would see the strange glare that was slow to leave his eyes.

At last, turning to the crowd, he said, "I'm sorry that we were not ready. I'm sorry that we failed. I'm sorry."

With that, he fell, limp, into the pew across the aisle from Prest Gran.

Whispering came from all parts of the building, making the air a cauldron of confusion. Some of the men dared to go to the windows and open them enough for a peek outside, while their nearest-of-kin begged them to be careful. Hours passed this way, interrupted only when a Gestapo officer would occasionally enter, shout, "Heil Hitler!" and renew Schreckenbach's warnings.

Finally, when the sun was high, Schreckenbach himself returned to the church. He said, "We have searched your houses and have taken possession of all firearms. Nothing else has been harmed, for we have come not to injure you, but to prevent, as I said before, the British from using you as a means toward injuring the invincible Reich!" In a flurry of patriotism he shouted again, "Heil Hitler!" Calm once more, he continued. "I have been assigned to Bjerkely and shall re— main in command here. If you prove agreeable, you shall find me most cordial. If you do not—" He stared at the people for a long moment.

"We have taken Narvik," he continued. "We shall soon have Oslo. We have invaded the Danish mainland, with very little resistance, and our transports and ferries are landing men by the hundreds on the Danish islands. We do not wish to be unkind to Scandinavia, but we must release the world from British tyranny! Heil Hitler!"

He walked to the door, turned, and said, "Now you may leave the church. Remember, the town is policed by my men. No one must leave the town limits. No one must show any signs of violence. Let that be sufficient warning! Heil Hitler!"

He left.

As the people reluctantly stood, Prest Gran called to them, "Have faith! God bless you! Keep trusting ' Him! All things work together for good to them that love God! He will not fail us! He cannot fail!"

Slowly, like hunted animals venturing from their dens, the people left the church and moved toward their homes. Many hesitated at each secluded spot, often seeing in one of these secluded places the ugly proboscis of a machine gun.

Borghild tried to prime Bjarne into a trot. "Lars!" she pleaded.

"Better not run," he warned. "Some fanatical machine gunner might think it was good sport."

"But Lars?"

"He'll be all right!"

"Lars!" she cried when they entered the house. "Birgit!"

Both came toward them, and Birgit cried, "There were Nazis here!"

Lars broke in, "They searched the house! They took Sigurd's gun!"

"What does it mean?" Birgit stammered.

Taking Lars into her arms, Borghild sobbed, "Oh, it's so horrible!"

"Are they going to hurt us?" Lars asked.

At that moment Prest Gran entered and promptly summoned his family to prayer.

Three

BY AFTERNOON, the radio had given the news of the Danish surrender; news, too, of the bombing of Oslo's strategic Kjeller Airfield; the landing of Nazi forces by plane at Fornebo Field outside the capital city. And, lest some be quick to skepticism, they needed only to look overhead, where squadrons of Goering's Luftwaffe, following the fjord shoreline, darkened the sky. The slim torso of a Dornier 17, the ugly threatenings of a camouflaged Heinkel IIIK, flying low, or a Messerschmidt, could be seen among the war birds—spawned in the nests of Lieutenant General Ernst Udet, propagator of the great German Air Force. And nowhere was so much as one R. A. F. fighter, or a Norwegian plane, to challenge the flock of vultures—and that was not difficult to understand, for the British, like the Norwegians, had been caught unawares; and the Norwegians, with thirty-two planes in their navy, eighty-three planes in their army, had no match for these.

Prest Gran, pacing and praying, praying and pacing, was approached in his study by his daughter.

"Why have they taken us, Father?" she asked, as simply as a child asks the reason for pain. "Why hasn't Sweden been taken, too?"

"The North Sea," he said. "The fall of Denmark assures the Kattegat, and the fall of Norway would assure German control of the Skagerrak. Sweden is the prisoner, without conquest, of any nation that holds the Kattegat and Skagerrak. I can't say Sweden is pro-German, but—"

"Her iron ore has been vital to Germany's war program, hasn't it?"

"But," he reminded grimly, "that ore wasn't taken to Germany through the Baltic, but—"

"Through Narvik," she completed.

"We were neutral. That was not wrong. If only we had known how vicious the Nazis really are." He paused, before saying, "The ore could have gone the- Baltic route, from Loulea in the Upper Baltic Sea, but that is icebound four months of the year. We were not wrong, nor was Sweden... for bad we forbidden passage, we wouldn't have been fair neutrals. It was Germany, not Scandinavia, that turned traitor."

She smiled into her father's taut face, not knowing why she did, except to cheer him.

"What is Bjarne doing?" he asked.

"Listening to the radio," she whispered, "ever so low."

"But Schreckenbach has posted an order that no one listen to news broadcasts, except from German-controlled stations, and if any refuses to comply, his radio will be confiscated."

"Bjarne has hidden his portable in the basement, just in case. Let's go to the living room and see if he's heard any unusual news."

Bjarne looked up when they approached.

"News?" Prest Gran asked.

"Bad! Very bad!"

"What?" from Borghild.

"I just heard the report that three NOrwegian ships, manned by fifth columnists, were warned of the German fleet at one-thirty this morning, but," he bit the palms of his hands with the tight pressure against his fingernails, "the Norwegians were ordered not to resist and to put all men ashore without arms of any kind. Evidently," he flared, "Bjerkely isn't alone!"

"Vidkun Quisling," Prest Gran sighed, "had more faithful followers than we thought."

"Yes," Bjarne answered. "Tromsö radio warns every town to beware of citizens, faithful residents for many years, who may be secret Quislingers aiding the enemy."

"I don't know who that could be here," Borghild spoke hastily.

"Which station are you listening to now?" .Prest Gran asked Bjarne.

"Bodo. It's been off the air at least three times now but has come on the air again to report escaping bombings. The British Home Fleet was attacked along our southern coast this afternoon, I heard."

"What about Norwegian resistance?" Borghild asked.

"The Norwegians have organized for guerrilla warfare all the way from Oslo north. I," he looked up into her pretty eyes, as though asking permission, "ought to try to join—"

"No, Bjarne! Remember Schreckenbach's warning that no one is to leave town!"

"That's right, son," the minister put in.

Bjarne shrugged, "I'd like to know any Gestapo man who knows the woods around here better than I do!"

"But you have no firearms," Borghild added.

"The radio tells of men fighting with pitchforks, axes, anything they can find. I could find some kind of—"

"No, son," Prest Gran gave emphasis to Borghild's restraining hand on her fiancé's shoulder.

"But—"

Sigurd's characteristic footsteps came from the kitchen.

"Even the hens don't lay like they Ought to—heh!" he giggled. "You're listening to the radio, too, eh? So've I been."

"Be careful, Sigurd," his employer warned.

"Wouldn't mind much if I did get caught," he chuckled. "It'd be worth it just to let 'em know that we're not taking all their talk like a bunch of anemics! Good news on the radio," his eyes twinkled, "isn't there?" -

"Good news?" Bjarne gasped. "Not unless you're a Quislinger!"

"Quislinger!" Sigurd stared violently at Bjarne. "I've helped put more faithful Social Democrats in the Starting than you've had birthdays... almost as many, anyway!"

"What do you mean by good news, then?"

"We'll have those Nazis running home like tin canned dogs within a week! That's what I mean by good news!"

"I suppose," Bjarne laughed, "you're going to put on one of Birgit's dresses, grab a broom, and become Norway's Joan of Arc! Maybe you could have your hair dyed red and pass as a reincarnation of Freydis, and—"

"Bjarne!" Borghild scolded, as she laughed.

Sigurd laughed too, and so did Bjarne and the Prest.

"O. K.," Bjarne conceded, "what's the good news?"

"Maybe," Sigurd. began, "Quisling and his gang of traitors have taken over the telephones, telegraph and radio in Oslo, but he's a long ways short of taking over the government. Hitler had it in mind to march our King and the Parliament through the streets of Berlin, but he'll never do it!"

"Tell me!" Bjarne demanded. "The King has escaped, hasn't he?"

"Sure he has! Mr. Hambro and the whole government! But maybe they wouldn't have, if it hadn't been for a couple of thickheaded Nazi ship captains."

"Why?" Borghild prompted.

"I just heard on my radio, before I picked the eggs, that a retired Norwegian naval officer—they didn't give his name—didn't know, I guess—who lives on the mainland near Fort Oscarsborg Island went into action when he heard the report about the invaders. Well," the old fellow grew dramatic, gesturing with his withering but agile hands, "when he got the news that Raeder's fleet was bearing up the fjord, he went right to the fjord to see. Not a ship in sight—yet; so he gets into a boat and rows himself to the fort, himself and a few men to help him, to where those two old guns (that the museums have been trying to get) point their muzzles to the sea."

"Listen!" Bjarne demanded. "You aren't trying to put over one of your far fetched stories, are you? This is no time for nonsense!"

"Nonsense? Humph! You'll not think it's nonsense when I finish telling you what happened... unless you're a Quislinger."

"All right, go ahead.

"Well, the German battleship... uh... Butcher, I believe they said... came idling to within five hundred feet of the fort; he gave his men orders to fire. First one and then the other gun shot, point-blank at the big ship, and she went to the bottom of the fjord, full of German financial experts who were supposed to have plans for changing this country of ours. Another boat was badly hurt, too. Well, according to the radio, it was because that old seaman held up the Germans that the King and the government had time to get important things together and get away!"

"Sigurd!" Borghild thrilled. "Is that really true?"

"Ski me down the steepest trail in Norway without a pole if it isn't!"

"God be praised!" Prest Gran exclaimed.

"Already Norwegians are getting ski troops together and giving the Nazis enough hot lead to keep them hustling." Sigurd winked, "If my old joints weren't so well along in years, I'd like to get into the fight, so I would!" Shaking a teasing fist at Bjarne, he half laughed, as he shouted, "Even if I only had a broom to fight with!"

"I've got to get into action like that!" Bjarne exclaimed. "I've got to—"

"Easy, young fellow," Sigurd whispered. "I've got a better idea."

"What?"

"Why would these Nazis send a man like Schreckenbach here to take over a little place like Bjerkely?"

"That's what a lot of us would like to know."

"Well, I don't know either," Sigurd admitted, "but if you ask me, this Schreckenbach is a pretty valuable fellow to the Nazis."

"What does that matter?"

"Matter? They wouldn't assign him to police this town unless they had some big plans for around here, would they?"

"Say, I'm catching on! You mean they might use this for some sort of a base? I get it! Maybe this is to be a secret hideout of some sort, a place the British would never suspect!"

"The water at our fishing docks," Sigurd said, "is deep enough to float the Bremen. 'Twouldn't surprise me none if there was a submarine or two in there while the Nazis sailed up the fjord, just in case they'd be needed."

"Submarine! Maybe you've got something there, Sigurd!"

"My idea is this," Sigurd continued, "that if Bjerkely is to be a key spot for the Nazis, it's up to us to make things hot for them . . . . make all the trouble we can. There's got to be wise heads for the job... and big husky fellows like you! Besides, Bjarne, there's still sort of martial law around here, and that makes it pretty dangerous to try anything right now. Soon's we learn the spots where Schreckenbach has men watching the town, we can arrange some escapes... for information, now that the telephone is taken over by Quislingers. Maybe we'll need to get dynamite... and guns, too, if necessary."

"Sigurd!" Bjarne extended his big hand. "You're a smart man! You've got some great ideas!"

"You certainly have!" Prest Gran added proudly.

Heavy feet came from the front entrance, and Schreckenbach appeared.

"You didn't ring!" Borghild scolded.

Schreckenbach blushed, bowed, and in soft tones, apologized, "I am sorry. Please forgive, won't you? My work demands so much of me, and I am but one man. I cannot waste time, even to ring a bell. But," he bowed again, "I will always apologize when I have offended those so charming!"

Bjarne cleared his throat, as he switched off the radio, and was relieved when he knew that he had not been apprehended.

Sigurd laughed, "Didn't know you catered to anybody but Quislingers!"

Schreckenbach was too absorbed with gazes at Borghild to glare at the self-styled wit.

But Sigurd, who would risk his one neck for as many laughs, followed through with, "Is Hitler that polite?"

"Sigurd!" Borghild scolded.

Schreckenbach was very pleased.

Borghild was sorry she had said anything. She bowed very faintly and left the room. Bjarne followed her.

"You can help me, Prest Gran," the Gestapo leader said.

"Huh!" grunted Sigurd.

Prest Gran reprimanded his *dreng*, "Let's not make trouble."

Schreckenbach beamed, "You are a very wise man, Prest. I trust Norway has many like you."

"Don't misunderstand," the minister hurried, "I am not endorsing you!"

"I hardly hoped for so much… though you would, if you could only realize that I' am your friend."

Sigurd tried to keep it from Coming, but it came, and he asked quizzically, "Our friend, you are? Like Goebbels is of real Germans. When he was sick a few months ago, your German Propaganda Ministry Office was deluged with calls," he winked, "from coin-box phones in Berlin, so the callers could'nt be traced. The callers wanted to know how Dr. Goebbels was getting along, and when they were told he was recovering, they'd say, 'That's too bad,' and hang up. Sure, you're our friend!"

"Swine! I have authority from the Leader to silence babblers like —"

"Sigurd!" said Prest Gran. "Let's hear what he has to say!"

Again Schreckenbach bowed. "Your wisdom humbles me, sir!"

"I can be courteous to all," the minister said, "even to my enemies." Magnificently, he added, "Jesus was to His!"

There was heavy silence for a long moment.

"I will listen," the pastor prompted.

"Thank you. We have invaded you," Schreckenbach began, "not like the British, who are wolves in sheep's clothing, but—though you think me strange to say it— we have invaded as sheep in wolves' clothing. We do——"

"Sheep?" Sigurd chirped. "Let's hear you bleat! We've heard the wolf growl!"

"Swine!"

"Sigurd, would you go?"

He obeyed, menacing Schreckenbach from the corner of his eye.

"How can you bear him, Prest Gran?"

There was no answer.

"Our agents have found official documents proving that France and Great Britain intended to invade you and use you as a means toward attacking us."

"But, Mr. Schreckenbach, isn't it as easy for the allies to strike at Germany through France... if they are the offending nations?"

"Blockade, sir! That strangled us during the last war, but," he beamed, "the lesson, though costly, was well learned!"

"Neither England nor France has shown any signs of aggression since the Treaty of Versailles."

"Why should they? They had us crushed, like brutes subjecting an injured foe! England ruled the sea! Her dirty Union Jack never knew a setting sun! I tell you, Prest, they are the wolves in sheep's clothing! And to keep you from their lethal clutches, the Führer was forced against his will to send us as sheep in wolves' clothing. Believe me! We want to befriend you! But because you wouldn't let us, we must come violently!"

Prest Gran said much by his silence.

"Your government refused our demands... our earnest pleas to be permitted to protect you from British tyranny, and—" he stopped abruptly. "But that is for historians in the free world soon to be born! I must get to my point. I have tried to appeal to Hunseid, the mayor, but he is so turned against me for our... our... our," he cleared his throat, "treachery—"

"He is a very faithful citizen, I am sure."

"And so I appeal to you, Prest Gran. You seem to understand human nature, as few whom I have known. I am most fortunate to have you in the populace assigned me, for," he hesitated first, "I have hopes that, through your mediation, I can reach the hearts of the people of Bjerkely... and get them to think sanely, and—"

"Stop!" Prest Gran said, holding out a restraining hand. "You are building false hopes!"

"But_"

"I cannot use the sacred position God entrusted to me to—"

"But, Prest Gran, it is for the good of your people!"

"Germany was the fountainhead of the Reformation, but Germany is also the source of what we know in theological terms as Modernism—a departure from the fundamental teachings and principles of the inspired, infallible Word of God. My work is to preach Christ, crucified for the sins of the world! If Germany had turned to my Christ—instead of to the philosophy of what I called Modernism—the horrible Nazi monster would neVer have appeared!"

"We are... purging... this religious radical from Germany, by ridding—"

"You are purging Germany of the true ministers of the Gospel, too, aren't you? Of men like Niemöller?"

Schreckenbach was silent, as his face reddened, then paled.

"The purge—"

"Not exactly a purge, Prest Gran," Schreckenbach tried to explain. "In *Mein Kampf*, the Führer said, 'I am fighting for the Lord's work.' You see, we aren't pagan. We—"

"One moment," Prest Gran smiled, "but, you see, I have also read *Mein Kampf*. Adolf Hitler said, 'By warding off the Jews, I am fighting for the Lord's work.' Isn't that correct?"

"The Jews aren't the Church!"

"But a Jew is the Rock, on which that Church was built! He is the King of the Jews, and one day He is coming back to rule them as the Prince of Peace! He shall rule the world! He is the central figure of the Book which even outsells *Mein Kampf* in Germany!"

Once more Bruno Schreckenbach was mute.

"You see, I want you to know that I understand you quite well. I have studied Nazism. I have read from Nazi pens that Christianity conflicts with your purposes, because it puts all races on a common level. Christ is the great leveler. To Him, all have sinned, . and come short of the glory of God, and so all need to find salvation in Him. I read Hans Weidler's brutal attack upon the Cross, when he said, 'Can there be anything lofty about a religion Whose God came into this world only for suffering and who died on the Cross the ignominious death of a criminal?' I read Wagner's attack upon our Book, that 'Adolf Hitler's books and speeches are our Sermon on the Mount.' Your leaders call Christianity an Asiatic superstition, an enemy of the Nazi State."

Schreckenbach cleared his throat; that was all.

"The Church and the Jew are God's human means toward carrying out His divine program upon earth."

"The Jew?" Schreckenbach burst forth.

Without losing stride, Prest Gran continued, "God made a covenant with Abraham, a promise that from his loins would come a great nation—the Jews. God said, *I will make of thee a great nation, and I will bless thee, and make thy name great; and thou shalt be a blessing: and I will bless them that bless thee, AND CURSE HIM THAT CURSETH THEE: and in thee shall all families of the earth be blessed.* You see," he smiled, "Hitler was right when he said that by fighting the Jews he was fighting for the Lord's work, because anti-Semitism is God's means of bringing the Jew out of the nations of the earth so that they will be ready to go to Palestine to meet their King, the Lord, Jesus Christ! Isaiah prophesied of anti-Semitism,"Mr. Schreckenbach, for he wrote, *Thus saith the Lord God, Behold, I will lift up mine hand to the Gentiles, and set up my standard to the people: AND THEY SHALL BRING THY SONS IN THEIR ARMS, AND THY DAUGHTERS SHALL BE CARRIED UPON THEIR SHOULDERS.* How else could God get His' people back to their native land to meet their King?" Then he quietly concluded, "Wouldn't you think me a fool, if I were to subject myself to your program, or urge my people to submit to your program... when I know that yours is doomed to failure... and His, whom I serve, shall emerge triumphant?"

"But—"

"What you need is to have the scales of Nazi fanaticism removed from your eyes, a miracle the Great Physician will perform if you will exercise saving faith in His atoning blood! Until you do, you will never be happy... no matter how victorious your quests may seem!"

Bruno Schreckenbach's arrogance seemed to waste away, until he was like a cremated corpse needing only a pin-prick to reduce it to the size of an urn. His eyes twitched nervously, seeking escape. And his hands fumbled with the legs of his immaculate uniform trousers.

"Do you agree with me, Mr. Schreckenbach?" Prest Gran asked, as a father addresses his, son.

Then the storm burst. Schreckenbach flared, "I, didn't come for a sermon! My orders, as an agent 'of' the Reich, are to subject Bjerkely, and I intend to carry out my orders! If you want to spare your people misery, you'll cooperate with me!"

"Need we come to words like this?"

"I'm sorry, Sir. My temper... pardon, please."

Prest Gran smiled.

"I am permitting you to go ahead with your church services, of course."

"No power on earth," Prest Gran reminded, "can hinder God's people from worshiping."

"But we could close your church!"

"Yes... you could."

"Next Sunday," he began boldly, "I want you to preach a sermon... or bring into the sermon you have prepared... warnings against belligerency. Tell your people that their rights will be respected, as far as possible, if they in return will not be obstinate."

"Tell me, what is your purpose in occupying Bjerkely?"

"The—"

"Aren't you a valuable man to be wasted by the Nazis in a small hamlet like this?"

"I am not being wasted! There—" he stopped, as though about to say something best kept unspoken, then calmed and continued, "is a purpose in occupying Bjerkely. It is a very important purpose, so important that no one will be permitted to leave Bjerkely to report it to the outside world. I tell you that, Prest Gran, so that you may more intelligently warn your people. I will prepare some rules for you to present to your people Sunday."

"What will they be like?"

"I will let you word them as you wish, if you don't alter the subject of the decrees."

"But—"

"This is Wednesday, isn't it? You shall have my statements by tomorrow evening, or Friday morning at the latest."

"But—"

Bruno Schreckenbach's eyes hid behind slits. "I shall attend the worship service personally Sunday morning."

"Then I can assure you that you will hear a message from the Word of God."

"And I shall also hear a message from the Reich to the people of Bjerkely!" Clicking his heels, Schreckenbach raised his hand in the Nazi salute and shouted, "Heil Hitler!"

Then he left.

"We heard!" Bjarne whispered, as he and Borghild entered the room when the outside door slammed.

"Sigurd was right, then," Borghild said, "about Bjerkely being strategic!"

"I'm glad we learned!"

"Yes," Prest Gran sighed. And then, "The future suggests much, but we don't dare to fear."

He left, to find seclusion in his study. For an hour, he searched his worn Bible, feeding his weary soul, refreshing its parched lips.

Then, after a brief prayer, he went to the window to watch the sunset. It was early in the afternoon, but the sun slipped into its winter bed early. He watched it sink into the west. He loved that sun! He had been north, where, during the long summers, the farmers plant their crops at sunup and harvest them at sundown. He had read his Bible outdoors at midnight. Yes, he loved that sun! But now it made him a trifle fearful, as, almost touching the horizon's crest. it cast weird shadows, grotesque and fantastic, of the *stabbur* (where the winter supply of farm foods was stocked) and the sheds and the church and the town.

Soon it made shadows of him—kneeling by the window like a fearless Daniel!

Four

THURSDAY CAME, and though many had had their radios confiscated by a Gestapo raid, news got about to all who would listen that the British had made a raid on Narvik; a five-hundred-mile sea battle raged along the entire coast; six German transports had been sunk in the Skagerrak by British submarines.

And so Thursday passed.

It was not until Friday morning that the little town felt the first real sting of Nazi occupation.

Breakfast was over in the Prest's home. Bjarne, who had given up hope of leaving Bjerkely at the present, was uptown for food. Lars still slept. Borghild and her father sat near the fireplace.

Planes roared overhead—laden with troops, was the rumor—but neither of them bothered to look outside until the roaring faded away.

Then Borghild went to the window, and said, "Beautiful Norway! This is a poor scene for things like this!"

Her father sighed.

As she stood, skipping her gaze over the *bakke* to the horizon where, a few miles farther on, they grew into the mountainous Swedish border, all of Norway loomed before her. She thought of. its rocky shorelines, on whose granite stairs she had stood and watched the Gulf Stream blend into the magnificent fjords. More than once her summer vacation had taken her cruising where the sea cuts between snow-capped mountains and penetrates into fjords as deep as the mountains are high—scenic caverns that eternally exclude direct visits from a sun ray in some of their narrowest crevices.

She had left the skerries of Bergen for the cruise northward, where huge fingers of rock taper into verdant tips which match colors with the sea. She had stood where snow-topped mountains, their sides patched by farms, look down on twisting fjords, whose waters are dark blue where they lie in the shadows, pale green where a shaft of sunlight sifts through a pair of peaks, lathering with foam when waterfalls whip them into fury. Waterfalls! Three-fourths of her beloved Norway was crumpled with mountains, edifices of stone bedecked with waterfalls whose chattering lips are the voice of the nation's beauty. She had watched the rivers, short and rapid when running eastward, accelerate in force until they were almost as lively as waterfalls; she had seen them prance in tandems through ravines, lope peacefully among green valleys, cavort over rocky rapids, and come to rest in those deep lakes which, together, cover more area than the cultivated land.

And she had been to Norway's homes—to the valley dwellings —some beside mountains so steep that she had seen the white tops through the chimney above the fireplace! She had been in the farm dwellings, alive with the bustle of summer, calm with the repose of winter and a stocked stabbur. And she had been to the cities, too— to Bergen, where it rains so much that horses are said to be afraid of any pedestrian who does not carry an umbrella;lto modern Oslo near by, with its cobbled streets in whorled designs, its smart shops, its gay sidewalk cafés where nasturtiums spend the summer in flower boxes; to Trondheim, the wooden city, with its great cathedral; to the old city, Hamar; to nautical Svolvaer, capital of the Lofoten Islands.

Norway! Her Norway! But not hers any longer, for a thief had come to steal it from her! The thought of that frightened her, and she screamed.

"Borghild!" Her father ran to her. "What's the matter?"

"Oh, I—I'm sorry, Father. I was... thinking." She forced a river of tears upstream, and swallowed hard.

Prest Gran placed his arm about her shoulders. "God knows all about it, dear."

"I know, but it's so hard to understand sometimes."

"Maybe God doesn't want us to understand. Faith works best when one doesn't understand."

"Thank you, Father," she smiled. "You help me so much."

Planes were coming again, so they left the window. But before they had time to again sit by the fire, Bjarne burst breathless upon them.

"I tell you," he shouted, "we've got to do something!"

"Bjarne, what's the matter?"

"Quick," Prest Gran urged, "what's happened?"

Bjarne stared at them through eyes which had become bloodshot since he left the house a few moments before.

"Bjarne!" Borghild pleaded. "What's wrong?"

"Five boys from the town—Sverre, Olaf, Einar, Trygne and Finn—tried to escape last night! They wanted to join the Norwegian forces! They! They! Oh, we've got to do something!"

"Bjarne!"

"They've been killed! Shot by Gestapo sentries!"

The first real sting of Nazi occupation had come!

"Sverre, Einar and Trygne were new converts from my last confirmation class!" the minister. gasped. "Olaf and Finn were— Bjarne, are you positive?"

"Schreckenbach's men laid their bodies on the snow at the square... with a sign at their feet that says: WE DO NOT WANT THIS TO HAPPEN AGAIN!"

"How terrible!" Borghild wept.

The door chimes sounded.

"Parents of the children, perhaps," Prest Gran sighed. "Dear Lord, give me words of consolation for them."

Bjarne offered, "I'll go to the door," and went.

It was Schreckenbach.

"Good morning," he said. "You haven't gone back to your paper in Oslo?"

"Murderer!" Bjarne glared, trying hard to discipline his fists. "You'll get your—"

"I came to see Prest Gran," Schreckenbach interrupted, brushing past the reporter.

"Sir!" The minister came to the hall. "What have you done?"

"Done? Have I done something?"

"Done something?" Prest Gran shouted. "Is it only routine for you to take the lives of five fine young—"

"That wasn't my fault!"

"They didn't commit suicide!" Bjarne dared.

"You can't blame me for that!" Schreckenbach insisted. "I kept my part of the bargain! They didn't keep theirs! They were safe as long as they didn't transgress my orders! I had warned them! What else was there to do?"

"How do you ever expect to win the friendship of Norway—if you think you could ever convince us now that this is your motive! —by atrocities like that?" Prest Gran asked.

"I am an obedient servant of my Führer," Schreckenbach blurted, "and I must rigidly perform all of my duties!"

"But you—"

"Sorry, but I'm very busy. Here," he said, handing an envelope to the minister, "are the items you are to present to your people Sunday morning."

With that he left.

Bjarne glared at the spot where the Gestapo leader had stood, and his clenched fists suggested that he was sorry he had not used them. Borghild, who had gone into the kitchen when the Nazi came, returned. Prest Gran, his head bowed, shed tears.

"I promise to avenge their deaths," Bjarne pledged, still staring at the spot, "if I have to keep that promise with my life!"

"Five boys," the minister mumbled, "five of Bjerkely's best young men. Why were they so impatient? Why couldn't they wait until God has shown His will more clearly? Why can't—"

"What's in the envelope, Father?" Borghild interrupted.

"The demands," he said.

"That Schreckenbach said you must read Sunday?"

He nodded, as he began opening the envelope. "Shall I read them?" he asked.

"Please."

He read, "One: All townspeople must consider all Germans as friends and treat them cordially. Two: Acts of violence will be punished with the maximum judgment of death. Three: No one must go near the town limits. Death is the certain penalty of all who are caught making the attempt. Four: No one may go near the fjord, including the town docks, without special permission. Five: If addressed by one of the Gestapo agents with the Nazi salute and 'Heil Hitler,' all natives, regardless of sex or social rank, must reciprocate."

"You... are to read that in church?" Bjarne asked.

"I'm supposed to."

"But why ask you?" Borghild asked. "Why can't he post those demands, as he has posted others similar to them?"

"He knows the spiritual quality of our people. He knows they trust me... so much," the Prest's eyes grew moist, "that if I were to ask them to be traitors, I believe they would obey me." The moisture made his eyes glow, as he added, "But I shall always urge them to be loyal to our beloved Norway!"

The door chimes sounded again. Leif Hunseid was admitted.

"Have you heard?" he asked.

"Yes, Leif, we have heard."

"What shall I do, Prest Gran? Shall I resign from my office? I can't go on this way! I can't see the people—"

"No," Prest Gran interrupted firmly, "don't resign! Be patient. The war hasn't been lost yet. Things are moving swiftly in favor of the enemy, the news is bad, but our God is greater than any circumstance!"

"Yes, but—"

"You have faith in God, haven't you, Leif?"

"Y—Yes... I... uh... yes, but—"

"You must have faith!" the minister emphasized. "Not faith that is born of fear, but faith that is childlike trust in the atoning blood of the Lamb of God! Have you that faith?"

Another interruption came from the door.

Five men entered, each a parent of one of the slain youths.

Their minister extended his hands the way he did each Sabbath when he gave the benediction. "My sympathies, dear friends! Jesus says, Come unto me, all ye that labor and are heavy laden, and I will give you rest."

"They've killed our boys!" one of them wailed.

Another, too furious for tears, shouted, "If we had guns!"

"Patience, men, patience! Jesus was as a dumb lamb before the shearers, but He, not Pilate and the Roman soldiers and the apostate Jews, won the victory!"

"But they've killed our boys! How can we sit back and not do anything?"

"There is nothing that can be done... now," Prest Gran answered. "Perhaps you will have to wait long until you see justice, but—"

"Our sons! Killed!" one who had been only sobbing now shouted. "That fool named Schreckenbach should pay for this!"

"Vengeance is mine; I will repay, saith the Lord," Prest Gran said. "Today we are the underdog. Tomorrow may tell a different story, but until that tomorrow comes, our violence would only incite more trouble... It has been that way in Poland."

"You are right," one of the men agreed, "but it is so hard to just sit back when our sons—" Sobs finished the sentence.

"Yes," Prest Gran said softly, laying his hand on the father's shoulder.

"We," one of the men hesitated, "came to make arrangements for—"

"The funeral?" the minister completed. "Do you wish the boys buried from one service?"

"Yes. Schreckenbach sent a man to tell us that we cOuld have the funeral Sunday afternoon." He bit his lip, before saying, "We ought to defy him and have it Monday!"

"That would be of little use," Prest Gran Said.

"We'll have it Sunday," the parent too angry for tears said. Shaking his fist, he added, "We ought to put a Gestapo dog in each casket, and one on top of each to hold down the lid!"

Prest Gran frowned and shook his head. "Jesus said, Love your enemies, bless them that curse you, do good to them that hate you, and pray for them which despitefully use you, and persecute you. These men are spiritually blind. We could do them no greater service than, by our lives, pointing them to Him who is able to make them see their sins."

One of the fathers exclaimed, "You are a great man, Prest!"

And the Prest answered, "I have a great God, who, even in His wrath, deals loving blows."

There was silence, except for heavy breathing and muffled sobs —fought back to add to internal agony.

"We shall have the memorial service Sunday afternoon, and I shall call at each of your homes before nightfall. Be brave, men! And be patient!"

"Thank you," they said, and turned to leave.

"God bless you, men! Take your souls to Him who cares, and He will bear your burdens for you!"

They left.

"Poor people!" Borghild choked. "The mothers! Dear women, their hearts must be broken."

"It is hard."

"If only we could do something!" Bjarne stormed.

"We can pray... and ask God to guide" us."

"Father is right, Bjarne."

"Yes... I know he is."

Silently they stood, like mourners at a grave.

Sigurd entered with a rush, shouting, "Have you heard about Einar, Finn, Sverre—"

"Yes," Borghild interrupted, "we have."

"Gunnarson ought to put a sign in the Window of his mortuary: WE CATER TO NAZIS AND WOULD RATHER DO BUSINESS WITH THEM THAN WITH NORWEGIANS!" Sigurd said.

"This is no time for jesting, Sigurd."

"I'm serious, Prest Gran. If the killing of five of our best young men wouldn't make anybody serious—"

Bjarne interrupted, "Prest Gran has more than that to make him serious."

"More fellows shot?" Sigurd demanded.

"No, but—"

"What then?"

Borghild informed, "Father has been given a list of five demands from Schreckenbach which he is to ask the people to observe."

"In a sermon?"

"Yes, Sunday morning."

"What are they?"

Prest Gran handed the sheet to his *dreng*.

Sigurd pulled out a pair of horn-rimmed glasses, and, cocking his head so he could use the bottom lens, read the writing silently.

"Are you going to?" he asked, when he looked up.

"What else can I do, Sigurd? I don't want to be the cause for more violence."

"B—But—"

"God knows how I would much rather not have to read them. My duty is to preach the Word, and—"

"Heh!" Sigurd brightened, as though he were deluged with an inspiration. "I'd better be moving along."

"Sigurd!" Prest Gran demanded. "What are you going to do?"

"I won't meddle with Schreckenbach... not," he winked, "directly. But I don't exactly plan to sit back and let him have his way without a speck of trouble."

He walked toward the door.

"Don't be foolish, Sigurd. It's no use for us to—"

"Sure," he chirped, "I know they call me the town clown, but this time I've got serious business on my mind."

"I warn you, Sigurd!"

"Heh!" he chirped again, as he left them. "What would one less old-timer my age matter? But I don't think they'll hurt me any. I'll be gentle! Heh! Heh! Sure, I'll be gentle to Schreckenbach!"

Five

SABBATH CAME—but there was no rest.

Prest Gran was in his study before dawn, because he had been there since dusk.

"Oh, God," he had prayed intermittently, "how can I use Thy house for things like this? Would it be profane?"

But there seemed to be no answer, no peace that came to give him assurance that he had his Master's will in the matter. Yet, in spite of the fact that he went nervously from the Bible to Schreckenbach's demands to his knees, he had peace—a calm assurance that all things would be well.

Perhaps it was a coincidence that he was fingering a copy of Neville Henderson's Failure of a Mission on one of the library shelves, when he determined that, by the grace of God, this mission would not fail!

There was a tapping at his door.

"Who?"

"Bjarne."

"Come."

"You haven't slept," Bjarne said, as he entered.

"This may be our Gethsemane," he smiled, "so I must not sleep."

"You bear a heavy burden, Prest Gran."

"I share a heavy burden," he corrected, "with my Lord!"

Bjarne smiled, then sobered, as he said, "I haven't been able to sleep, though I retired... thinking of you and the tremendous job you have today. The service this morning... the funeral this afternoon. I was at the square before curfew last night. The people's faces were foreboding. There wasn't a smile, and few even spoke. I asked what was wrong... if it were anything special... but no one would answer me."

"The people are disturbed by the deaths."

"And," Bjarne said, "if they make more trouble, there'll be more funerals."

"We shall try to prevent that".

"If there's ever anything I can do—" "Bjarne began to offer.

"Pray, my boy!"

"I have, sir." His eyes met the Prest's without wavering. "Borghild and I spent much time in prayer together last night."

"God bless you, Bjarne!"

"I—I," he swallowed hard, "I've been a bit flippant with my faith, but I'm on solid ground now! You've proved that faith in God is real!"

Prest Gran smiled radiantly.

"You're reading those demands this morning?"

"I'm not sure what to do, Bjarne. I—I can't seem to be sure of God's leading... I'm only sure of one thing —that God will undertake for me and lead me in What is best."

"Schreckenbach! I wonder if all Nazis are like him."

"All Nazis, I have no doubt, Bjarne, though I still haven't lost faith in the German people. But," he. sighed, "I'm sure there are many like those who are here. If Hitler had been killed in the Munich Beer Hall blast, there would have been someone as vile as he to take his place."

Neither of them spoke, until, after a brief silence, Bjarne said, "I'm afraid Schreckenbach is going to cause a lot of trouble in Bjerkely."

"And yet, when I speak to him of spiritual things, I see a hunger in his eyes—a deep longing for the realities of which I speak. Maybe —"

"Seems like," Bjarne blurted, "a fellow like that is beyond the grace of God."

"God's grace embraces the world, Bjarne, and all who will may accept it. Whosoever shall call upon the name of the Lord shall be saved. That about includes everyone, doesn't it?"

Bjarne seemed puzzled.

"When Christ died on the Cross," Prest Gran continued, "He bore the sins of all the world! However great these evils may seem, Christ has paid the pardon for them! But men refuse that pardon, and so they continue... steeped in sin."

For a moment, the minister turned the leaves of his Bible. Bjarne went to the window and watched morning gown the out-of-doors. In the distance he could see the cemetery, where five graves, dug the evening before, were starkly black against the carpet of snow... thus suggeSting many things—fearful things, distressing things. It was not yet light enough to hide the glow of windows, and he saw the homes of those who had been killed, homes in which lights had burned all night, for the occupants were too grieved to sleep.

"I listened to my radio this morning," he said, turning inward.

"More bad news?"

"Some. Nazi soldiers have been tying men and women to their cars as shields, and parachutists, who've taken shelter in farmhouses, use women and children to protect them from enemy bullets. I tell you, sir, that makes the blood cake in my veins!"

"Yes, Bjarne... I know how you feel."

"The radio report said, though, that Norwegian volunteers to Finland are already returning to fight at home." And in the same breath, he added, "I'd give my best arm to get out there with them!"

"There may be work here."

"I'm almost counting on it!" Bjarne beamed. Then he continued, "Dive-bombers even machine-gunned the Royal Party and members of the Cabinet, and the only shelter they had was under spruce trees."

"Is that true?" the Prest demanded, giving emphasis with a quick jerk of his body.

"According to the radio, and," Bjarne shrugged, "we Norwegians haven't had much education in the wiles of propaganda!" He took a step nearer the minister. "Can you tell me why the Nazis would want to kill our King?"

Prest Gran stood, six inches taller than he had ever stood before, it seemed. "They would kill our King for the same logical reason that the Athenia was sunk... and Jewish wives answer night-tappings at their doors, to be given a package by some Gestapo agent, a little sack of ashes that is all that remains of their husbands... for the same reason Poland and Czechoslovakia have been raped... if there's logic in any of this! This earth has given birth to a Frankenstein, Bjarne! Thank God the omnipotent Saviour was born twenty centuries before, or we would have reason to be fearful!"

Before Bjarne's eyes, Prest Gran had been changed into a personality he had never seen before—a vivid illustration of the Biblical request, Be ye angry, and sin not; for the usual softness that characterized him had become ruddy; his eyes were like two hot bullets, caught in flight by a high-speed camera that retained every evidence of their frenzied quest for action; his brow furrowed and smoothed, like the heavy waters of a stormy fjord; his lips labored to refuse utterances; and his thin hair fell as the baldachin over the throne of an indignant monarch who needed only to expend a dozen words to make right the atrocity—until one would think the kindly Prest was a direct descendant of the stock that begat Norsemen like Eric Bloody-Axe, Harald Creycloak, and Rolf the Ganger.

Then, suddenly, the former personality returned again, and gradually his amiable face gave mooring to a smile.

"God could remove the enemy with one word from His mouth," he continued, "and he would... if there were a better way of drawing His people's faith more closely to Him."

Bjarne never forgot those words!

"I pray for grace to see as you see," he whispered.

"A thousand years from now, Bjarne... much less than that for me, and even you, of course... it won't matter how the enemy has treated us... but it will make a great difference then as to how we now take the burdens and trials God has entrusted to us."

Only once had Bjarne stood beneath the Romanesque transept of the cathedral at Trondheim, where the Gothic nave and choir also look down upon the mellow-lighted pews and the tomb of St. Olaf, and the sacrosanct atmosphere had demanded silence of him.

He felt that way now.

Nothing was said until the door chimes sounded.

"I'll go," Bjarne offered.

Through the semi-stained outlook on the heavy door, he saw that it was a Gestapo officer; so he was careful that the radio was turned off before boldly opening the door.

"A message from Bruno Schreckenbach to the Prest," the Nazi said.

Bjarne took it and delighted to shut the door in his face.

"From Schreckenbach," he said, when he reached the study.

Prest Gran opened it, read it aloud:

Esteemed Sir:

I have received a message from headquarters in my beloved fatherland asking me, along with others in my position, to do my best in winning the confidence of the Norwegian people, thus restoring our long cherished friendship.

Your cooperation will be appreciated, and our mutual God will reward you.

Most humbly,

Bruno Schreckenbach

Then he read it silently.

"What do you make of it?" Bjarne prompted.

The minister laughed.

"Propaganda?"

"Could it be anything else, Bjarne, when the words"confidence" and "friendship" are used?"

Birgit called from outside, "Pardon, sir, but you asked breakfast early this morning."

"Oh, yes," arising, "thank you, Birgit. Are Borghild and Lars up?"

Birgit stood in the door to say, "She is, but she asked that Lars be served at the usual hour."

"That's imposing on you, but Borghild will help. He needs his sleep. It won't keep you from attending the service... the delay, will it?"

Borghild had returned to the kitchen.

Sigurd was in the dining room when they arrived. Though some did not, Prest Gran had always insisted that his *dreng* eat at his table.

"Good morning, Sigurd."

"Nice morning," Bjarne added.

"Morning," Sigurd sighed. It was as noticeable that the grin was gone from his face as it is When one has caught a man without his false teeth.

Borghild entered, smiling in spite of the shadows that brooded about her eyes.

"It is ready," Birgit announced.

Everybody found his usual chair.

"Father," the minister prayed, "bless this food. We thank Thee for the rest of the night, for the promise of guidance for the day. In Jesus' Name, amen."

A platter of *stegt torsk* was convoyed by crisp toast, jam, scrambled eggs and milk. But all were slow to start the invasion.

"Sigurd," the minister smiled, "didn't you work up an appetite this morning?"

"Not very hungry."

Prest Gran teased, "Don't let me see you pull out your watch in church to remind me that it's dinner time."

Sigurd said, "Don't believe I can make it to church this morning."

"Are you ill?"

"A little under the weather, I guess?"

"What—"

Birgit added, "I'm not feeling so well myself."

"Well, now, that's too bad."

Birgit coughed, and so did Sigurd—until it seemed they were contesting for valetudinarian honors.

"You two had better see Dr. Berg in the morning, if—"

"It'll pass over," Sigurd assured.

"Have some toast," Birgit inserted, hurrying to the kitchen, "there's plenty."

Prest Gran chuckled, "I've never yet seen a little cold keep Birgit home from the service."

And so the meal continued.

When the hour of the service arrived, the house became deathlike. Silence lurked everywhere, as though it kept vigil over sound to stab to death any that ventured appearance. Prest Gran, in his study for a last moment of prayer, wrestled with his thoughts, for it was work to pray.

Lars came to his door to remind, "Borghild says it's time to go, Father."

"Yes. Right away, son."

Birgit and Sigurd were not seen. "They've probably gone on," Borghild said, when Bjarne, Borghild, Lars and the Prest left the house and walked toward church.

"No stragglers this morning," Bjarne commented.

"Probably," his fiancée put in, "everybody is at church early... to hear the demands."

A heavy breath came from the third adult.

Then only the crunching of the snow.

And more deep breaths.

The edifice—a semi-replica of those medieval-born stave churches, with pagoda-like roofs and spires and *svalgangs* (narrow corridors) surrounding the building where ancient Norsemen met before and after the service—seemed to have changed the gesture of its spire from a beckoning hand to a restraining hand. But the group did not heed its warning, and when they reached the *svalgang* Prest Gran left the other three and went to the entrance to the pulpit study, where he could don his clerical attire.

Bjarne, Borghild and Lars entered the auditorium.

"Empty," Borghild whispered.

Pulling his sleeve above his wrist watch, Bjarne asked, "Is our time wrong?"

But the clock on the wall agreed with his; it was church time.

"I've never seen the church empty on Sunday morning... even if we had a blizzard," Borghild puzzled.

"Maybe people are waiting until the last minute," Bjarne said, "in case Schreckenbach—"

The door opened behind them, and Schreckenbach entered.

"Good morn—" he began to say; but changed to demand, "Where are the people?"

"That's what we'd like to know," Bjarne said quite cordially.

"Maybe they're late," Borghild said.

Schreckenbach bowed to her, smiled, and said, "Maybe." Moments passed, while they stood silently near the entrance, and no one came. Again he demanded, "Where are the people?"

Prest Gran came to the platform. He did not look toward the empty pews at first; instead, his attention was toward the silent organ, for he wondered why there was no prelude. Then he lOoked at the auditorium and shrunk back, surprised.

"Where are my people?" he asked.

"We don't—" Bjarne started.

But Schreckenbach broke in, "Is there conspiracy here?"

"Conspiracy?" Borghild scoffed. "What on earth do you mean?"

Prest Gran was not listening. Before him, on the communion railing, lay an envelope addressed to him in Sigurd's handwriting. He opened it. It contained a note, which he read.

> Dear Prest Gran,
>
> I have asked all of the people to stay away from church today, so you would not need to read Schreckenbach's demands.

Your dreng,

Sigurd

He was about to thrust the note inside his robe, when Schreckenbach advanced and demanded, "What is that?"

"It—"

"Let me see it!"

"It is not for you," he said indignantly.

"Let me see it!" Schreckenbach echoed.

"I—"

"In the name of the Gestapo!"

Boldly, Bruno Schreckenbach climbed over the altar railing and advanced toward Prest Gran who backed away.

"Give me—"

"It isn't yours, Mr. Schreckenbach! Aren't you a gentleman at all? Have you no sense of the sacredness of God's house?"

But Schreckenbach advanced, striking, with each step, fear into the Prest's heart, for he knew what would happen to Sigurd if Schreckenbach were to learn that he was the cause of the trouble. The Gestapo officer's hand was extended to grasp the note from him, when Bjarne was seen coming from the rear. Fear of more trouble struck Prest Gran's heart. Desperately, he slipped the note under the gold cross on the altar.

"Now you are challenging God," he said, with something of a smile.

Schreckenbach stopped. Once, twice, three times he tried to reach for the note, but each time he refrained. Then he stepped back.

"I don't need to read it," he snapped. "I'm no blockhead! Your people have stayed home from church to keep from hearing my demands! They can't do this and expect me to keep my peace! I'll —"

"Have mercy on the people, Mr. Schreckenbach!" Prest Gran pleaded, "Imagine yourself, if some one transgressed your rights! Try to—"

"Prest Gran!" Schreckenbach interrupted. "You will read those demands at the funeral for those five rebels this afternoon! And if the people aren't here, I'll know it's because you have told them to stay away, or," waving an arm at Bjarne, "that one of those here has conspired!" His eye fell on Borghild, and he blushed, but remained defiant and stormed out of the building, taking time to stop at the door, salute, and shout, "Heil Hitler!"

"Father!" Borghild came toward the front. "What shall we do?"

But the Prest didn't answer. He was kneeling, like a penitent sinner, at the railing, begging God for wisdom to understand.

Six

NO DINNER WAS PREPARED. No one wanted any.

Birgit and Sigurd tried to pry into the results of the strange service, but Lars, let alone the others, could not be bribed or persuaded to tell.

Afternoon came, bringing with it the hour of the funeral. Prest Gran went early to the church for prayer. Before he went back to head the procession, he saw that the auditorium was packed to capacity. And in the crowd of civilian clothes, it was not difficult to notice Gestapo uniforms.

He paused for one moment of prayer.

The organist chose one of Lindeman's sacred compositions for the funeral march—a sacred piece suggesting possibilities of hope and comfort and understanding.

Slowly, the sober Prest led the train of five caskets down the aisle. They were so laden with flowers that it was difficult to see any indications of social rank— though there were rich and poor going to their graves together.

While the caskets were lined. at the front, and the flowers arranged, once more the minister stepped into his side room.

"Father," he prayed, "how can I? How can I?"

A peace, mingled peace (like sweet nectar mixed with gall), came over him. Quickly, he drew Schreckenbach's demands from his notebook, and slowly he tore the paper into bits.

And then he wondered if he had done right, while knowing that he would do wrong to so desecrate the house of the Lord.

He went to his pulpit. A mixed quartet sang.

There was much sobbing.

When the song was finished, he brought the people to their feet with the motion of his hands.

"Let us pray," he said. "Oh, God, we beg Thee for Thy blessing upon this service. May it teach us of the horrors of war and make us eager for the Prince of Peace. May it remind us of death and give us a greater zest for eternal life, which is in Christ Jesus our Lord. May Thy blessing comfort those who mourn. Yet, let us not in our search for comfort neglect the ministry of admonition. Remind us once more of the wages of sin... and of the gift of God; of the darkness of eternal death... and of the brilliance of eternal life. In Jesus' Name, amen."

He read the obituaries.

Then there was another song... and more sobbing.

Prest Gran had never preached before as he did now. His voice seemed to borrow cadence from heaven and force resonance from hell. He sketched glorious pictures of Paradise and contrasted them with grim portrayals of perdition. He admonished and pleaded, incited and warned.

And then he concluded, "We must see life in its true sense. It is not the tale of our existence, with death as its climax. Life should not house all of our ambitions, our desires and our concepts. Life is but the means by which we are given entrance, through death, into eternity; it is the field whose bins lie beyond the grave; it is the mold in which our souls are cast—either into the likeness of Christ, or into the likeness of Satan whose henchmen lurk upon the earth in staggering numbers seeking those whom they can devour; it is the time allotted us," he paused for emphasis, "by the Creator to grasp the Pilot's hand and be lifted out of the depths of sin, across the storm-tossed sea of mortal existence, and onto the solid rock of eternal safety in the glories beyond!"

The mixed quartet sang again—one of the women becoming silent on the second verse of the hymn, the other joining her before its chorus. But no one noticed, for all eyes were drenched.

Prest Gran stepped down from the pulpit. He followed the last of the caskets to be wheeled to the *svalgang*. There he stood while the public mourners walked by. It was his custom.

Just before the doors were closed to the last of the public, Bruno Schreckenbach whispered from behind the minister, "Why didn't you read those demands?"

Prest Gran did not turn, nor did he answer.

Bruno Schreckenbach went out, and the doors were closed.

Prest Gran never shed tears at a funeral he conducted, for, through the years of his experience, he had learned to force his personal sorrows inward where they were unseen. But now, as he went to each of the five circles pivoted by a casket, the tears made channels of his furrowed face, and the only sympathy he could offer was the warmth of his hand and the strength of his smile... and the presence of his tears.

Mothers stroked the hands of their deceased sons. Sweethearts refused to look at the remains. Stalwart fathers wept more than the women. Brothers and sisters stared through parched eyes.

And then the lids were closed.

At the request of the relatives, unknown to Prest Gran, all flowers were removed from the caskets, and as they were borne from the building, each was draped with the Norwegian flag.

The minister led the procession, which passed through two thick lines of people from the church to the cemetery. He was fearful at first, lest the flags incite more difficulty with the Gestapo, but none of their officers was seen, and he proceeded boldly.

He did not look up to see the faces he passed, but if he had, he would have seen vengeance brooding among the tears, anger dethroning the portrayed agonies of sorrow. Men watched the procession, while those same eyes glared a defiant pledge that these had not died in vain. Mothers, through tightly drawn lips, were offering their sons, too, that Norway, and Bjerkely, might once more be free.

One by one the bodies were committed to the ground. It was a long procedure, but the kind Prest wanted none to be slighted.

When the fifth casket had been sprinkled with petals —for he would not permit dirt to be thrown on the flag —and he had said, "Dust thou art and unto dust shalt thou return," the distant roar of a plane, which no one had noticed, rapidly came closer. And before the crowd began to disperse, a Messerschmidt was snarling overhead, circling, dipping, then climbing upward.

Some of the men shook their fists. Some of the women screamed. But all were driven to panic when the fighter plane dived at the crowd, spitting a stream of machine gun bullets from its nose!

"Heavenly Father!" Prest Gran prayed, as he followed the mob toward the shelter of the church.

Borghild grasped his arm. Bjarne had hers.

The plane lifted from its dive, leveled and circled about the town and returned to the crowd. A few looked up as they ran, shouting for others to seek shelter while they themselves, confused, stumbled aimlessly.

Like a hungry hawk, the plane circled about the crowd, now thrust against the church with such impact that only a few could get in; then it dived; but no shots were fired, and it zoomed away. It did not return.

Gradually the people calmed enough for one voice to be heard above another.

Leif Hunseid called, "Let's file into the church orderly, people, so we'll be safe if that fool thing comes back!"

"He's flying away, Leif!" someone reminded.

"But he might come back," Hunseid insisted.

A woman cried, "Some were hurt! I saw them fall!"

Another added hysterically, "They're lying back there at the cemetery!"

The crowd surged toward the cemetery, except for a few of the shy who stayed at the church.

Bjarne, beside Prest Gran, exclaimed, "Sure enough! Must be a dozen bodies around the caskets! I thought maybe that Hun shot blanks!"

"Oh!" Borghild screamed.

Bjarne and the Prest thought it was because of the horrible sight of seeing the bodies slumped about the caskets, which had not been lowered. Then, seeing her run ahead, they, too, knew why she screamed.

"Lars!" Prest Gran shouted.

"Lars!" Bjarne echoed.

When they reached her, Borghild was kneeling beside her brother. "Lars," she pleaded, "are you hurt? Lars, talk to me! Lars! Lars!"

But he did not speak. And he did not open his eyes. And he did not move... There was not so much as a faint motion of the diaphragm.

"Lars, my boy!"

"Lars, old fellow! Are you hurt?"

"Your boy, Prest Gran?" It was Dr. Berg who had approached.

"Doctor... is he... Do you..."

"I'll see, Prest Gran," the physician, who had begun his practice in Bjerkely a quarter of a century before and had attended Lars' birth, said, as he knelt beside the boy.

"Doctor," Borghild pleaded, "is he..."

"I'm afraid so."

"No! My boy! My boy!"

"Lars!"

"Terrible!"

"My sympathies," the physician said, and hurried to answer the cries of others.

Tenderly, Prest Gran lifted the body of his boy into his arms. He did not see that a crimson stream left the side of his son and stained his pulpit robe; and had he seen it, he would not have done otherwise.

Lifting his eyes heavenward, he prayed, "Father! I thank Thee for taking him Home! He is so much more happy now! He is away from these horrible things! He is safe with Thee! I thank thee, Father! I thank Thee!"

He carried the remains home, not looking to the right nor to the left. There he laid the body on the bed where Lars had rested so many nights, and where his mother had so often soothed away his cares with tender caresses.

Seven

PREST GRAN did not release his vigil until Gunnarsen, the mortician, came for the body. Then he went to his study, and through the door, Bjarne and Borghild could hear his futile attempts to muffle the sobs.

"Sweetheart," Bjarne comforted, drawing Borghild to him, "your father is right. He's better off, now. It may be much worse here, before this is over."

"I know," she sobbed, "but it's so terrible. This morning he was with us, and this afternoon he is dead! Oh, Bjarne!"

"I never knew human beings could be so dirty! Machine-gunning a helpless crowd! Our friends! Not much!"

Borghild looked up at Bjarne, now, denying the tears. In the firm lines of her face he saw the tenacity of the immortalized Gudrid, mother of the first white child born in the Americas, whose feminine foot imprinted the shores of Greenland, Iceland, America and Italy; and there was the acceptance of any challenge from the future, like the heroine of Magnihild Haalke's Alli's Son, whose arms grew sinewy rowing over the waves from an island home to the mainland each day, so that little Elling might have the possibilities of an education; and, too, there was in her eyes the faith of Ingeborg, who, during the absence of her Viking hero, Frithjof, had been given to another, the king, but whose faithful waiting was rewarded with the delivering return of her lover; and, best, there was all the greatness of lovely Borghild, denying the tears!

"Yes," she smiled, "Lars is happy now! It is best!"

"Good girl!"

"Who will conduct the funeral?"

"I don't know."

They had not heard the study door open, nor the grief-stricken parent approach.

"I will," Prest Gran said.

"No!" Borghild protested.

"There is none other, and," he smiled faintly, "Lars would like for me to, I know."

Bjarne swallowed hard. Such faith does that to the strongest men, and he was not ashamed of the tears which were not checked.

"Father, how can you?"

"I can do all things through Christ which strengtheneth me."

Borghild wept on her father's coat lapel.

The door chimes sounded, and even their tones seemed to have been affected by the sorrow.

"I'll go," Bjarne said. At the door, he snapped, "Schreckenbach! You dog!"

"May I see Prest Gran?"

"If you'd come a few minutes earlier, you could have seen his son—the corpse of his son!"

Schreckenbach advanced, without saying more.

"Bruno Schreckenbach!" Prest Gran exclaimed.

Borghild shuddered but did not leave the room.

"Prest Gran," the Gestapo agent bowed, "Miss Gran... my genuine sympathies."

"Sympathies?" Borghild gasped.

Prest Gran spoke through gritted teeth. "How can you—"

Schreckenbach interrupted, "Prest Gran, I have been impressed by your fairness... your willingness to withhold judgment until—"

"But you can't expect," the minister broke in, "me to—"

"Please, Prest Gran! Don't let me be disappointed in my previous conception of you! Don't judge me harshly, until you have let me explain. Isn't that fair?"

"I'll listen."

"Oh, Father," Borghild flared, "it's no use! All he wants is to cover the filth of his—"

"Miss Gran," Schreckenbach bowed, "I have suspected in you the inherited wisdom of your esteemed father!"

She flew at him like a wounded bird. "Murderer! Trying to make right your wrongs, because you have control of—"

"Please, Miss Gran! Please! I beg of you!"

"Listen!" Bjarne could not continue his silence. "There are some things that can be explained, Mr. Schreckenbach! The Norwegians have always been quick to forgive! But when fiends—"

"Mr. Kolstad!" Bruno Schreckenbach pleaded. "Please! Please!"

"The Righteous Judge will treat all men fairly," Prest Gran arbitrated. "Why should we do less... even to those who injure us?"

"All right," Bjarne mumbled.

Schreckenbach gasped, "You are a very wise man, Prest Gran! I am humbled by your personality!"

"We will hear what you have to say," the minister said.

"I am indignant at what happened this afternoon," Schreckenbach began. "I was to report to our Norwegian headquarters immediately, if my demands were not read at... at," he cleared his throat, "the funeral. I endeavor to faithfully execute all orders, and so I contacted our headquarters." He paused, and his face twitched, before he continued, "I thought I was to report so that further orders could be given to me, but... I didn't receive instructions, and... when I asked my commanding officer what I should do, he asked if the crowd had left the cemetery. I told him they hadn't because," he swallowed hard, "because... there were," again he swallowed, "five to be buried. He cut me off immediately." Bruno Schreckenbach now took a deep breath. "He must have radioed to the fighter plane which attacked, because I was as surprised as you. I have protested to my commanding officer," he sought sympathy with the meek squint of his eyes, "at the risk of losing my rank with the Gestapo, but—"

"At least you admit," Bjarne snapped boldly, "that the Nazi method of subjecting a conquered people is rotten to the core!"

Schreckenbach jerked, and his eyes shot two hot streams of indignation at Bjarne.

"Let us be fair," Prest Gran urged Bjarne, "even though our enemy may not be. Go ahead, Mr. Schreckenbach."

"Thank you, Prest Gran. You are a very wise man!" He cleared his throat. "Death of my captives is never my objective. I don't want to harm anyone, and my honest ambition is to be fair in—"

"Don't want to kill anybody?" Bjarne broke his brief verbal fast. "I suppose your sentries were having a Norwegian *skytterlag*, and in their sport of shooting at targets, those five fellows happened to get in the way!"

"That was because they broke our martial law!" the Nazi defended. "My commands from Gestapo headquarters are that no one is to leave Bjerkely! And because it is so necessary that no one leave, the death penalty must be inflicted on any who make an attempt!"

"What would it matter if anyone did leave?" Bjarne asked. "There are no munitions, or other war work, projects here. This isn't a base of any kind that the Nazis are—"

Schreckenbach sparkled with pride. "The British don't know that Bjerkely is occupied. And we are going to see to it that they don't find out! As soon as the capture of Norway is complete, Bjerkely will become a very important cog in Germany's procedure to eliminate the vile British from Europe!"

Bjarne made careful note of Schreckenbach's boast.

"Of course," the Nazi continued, "you people don't approve of our demands! I can see, Prest Gran, why you didn't read those five points. I should have been more considerate and posted them, as I did the martial law order. But, you see, I thought that you could help to spare further difficulties for your people." He beamed, "You will approve, though, when historians reveal the truth after the war—that Great Britain would have made slaves of you, if you hadn't had us for your friends!"

Prest Gran looked at the floor. Bjarne glanced tensely at his clenched fists. Borghild covered her eyes with her pretty hands. Schreckenbach fidgeted.

"I extend my most sincere sympathy to you, Prest Gran, and to you, Miss Gran. I wish there were some way to make restitution, but... there isn't... now. After the war is over in a few months," his eyes sparkled again, "and you learn the truth, you will say," he became dramatic with softly spoken words, "that the death of the boy was well worth the sacrifice."

"Oh, you horrible brute!" Borghild screamed. "How can you say such things? Do you think we will believe that you really are sorry that Lars was murdered? Do you think we're such fools as to believe a lie like—"

"I can only tell the truth, Miss Gran, and pray that you will believe me! If you won't believe me, I shall be forced to wait until the day when my truthfulness will be vindicated."

Sobbing, Borghild ran from the room and ascended the stairway.

Schreckenbach sighed, following her departure with his eyes and lingering at the entrance to her exit.

Bjarne's eyes lingered on Schreckenbach. Then their eyes met in a moment of conflict.

"Don't you think," Prest Gran asked, "that it would have been better for the Nazis to have left Norway at peace? Don't you think that—"

"But we had to invade to pro—"

"God will judge all sins, Mr. Schreckenbach, except those which have been forgiven by the blood of Christ. The wicked shall be turned into hell, and all the nations that forget God, the Bible warns. Vengeance is mine; I will repay, saith the Lord. The Bible clearly says, Thou shalt not kill. No unrepentant murderer shall ever enter heaven! No sinner, who rejects Christ as his Saviour, will escape the merciful but violent judgments of God!"

"I...uh..."

"I can forgive the death of my son. On the Cross, Jesus prayed, Father, forgive them; for they know not what they do. It isn't easy to see him snatched from us, but... God knows. Lars isn't sorry for his death. Now," there was a lonesomeness, a longing, in Prest Gran's voice, as though he, too, would like to join his son, "Lars is in the presence of the Lord! Many times I've knelt by his bed and heard him pray, not a prayer he had learned but a prayer that lifted from his heart. He was only a boy, but he prayed the prayers of a mature saint. He knew whom he had believed! He had faith in Christ!" Quietly, he added, "That is what you need, Mr. Schreckenbach... faith in Christ."

"Uh—I—uh—"

"You've been blinded by Nazi fanaticism, caught in the clutches of mob frenzy! It is useless to try to subject people by cruelty! Goebbels said that it is foolish to think that any people want to rule themselves, but he is wrong! Power entrusted by one's subjects makes a leader humble, but power gained by greed and lust makes one arrogant; and it only incites the hatred of the subjected ones until they inevitably rise to crush the dominant aggressor! Nazism is doomed to fall, Mr. Schreckenbach! I warn you! No militant power that seeks to crush all that is right and raise the banners of evil can expect to survive! There's no alternative but failure! And if you would be wise, you would give your splendid life to Him and not waste it in the greedy programs of Nazism... programs as doomed to defeat as is Satan and all the armies of hell!"

"Defeat?" Schreckenbach tried to laugh, but it was a poor attempt. "The invincible Reich defeated? That isn't possible—"

"You forget my quotation from the Bible, Mr. Schreckenbach. The wicked shall be turned into hell, and all the nations that forget God. There never has been a nation, nor an individual, who succeeded in a belligerent contest against Almighty God! The angelic Lucifer tried it, and he became Satan! The Word of God says, Why do the heathen rage, and the people imagine a vain thing? The kings of the earth... take counsel together, against the Lord, and against his Anointed. That's one side of the picture, Mr. Schreckenbach, for that same chapter says, He that sitteth in the heavens shall laugh: the Lord shall have them in derision. Then shall he speak unto them in his wrath, and vex them in his sore displeasure. You can't defeat the ways of God! But you can accept His plan of salvation, performed in the death of Christ Jesus upon

Calvary's Cross, and be one of the company who walks in His ways! You can—" "

"I'm sorry, but I must go. You are very interesting, Prest Gran, and," he took a half dozen steps toward the door, "my sympathies! My deepest sympathies!"

He left.

Sigurd entered. There was no mirth on his face. There was the other extreme, the struggle with tears.

"It's all my fault, Prest Gran!" He bit his lips. "If I wouldn't have asked people to stay away from the morning service like I did, and—"

"I am as much at fault as you, Sigurd. I was the one who refused to read Schreckenbach's demands."

"Lars is dead!" Sigurd wept. "Why did it happen to a youngster like him? Why couldn't——?"

"It is best," Prest Gran comforted. "All things work together for good!"

"Yes, but—"

"No good thing will be withheld from them that walk uprightly. God wants our praise, not our complaints!" There was silence for a long moment.

Then Sigurd shouted, "I wish I could even the score with that Schreckenbach and—"

"God would have us pray for him!" the minister interrupted.

"But—but—"

Prest Gran stood like an animate portrait of Stoltenberg's masterpiece painting of a clergyman. Slowly, his countenance darkened, as he thought of the funeral, the machine-gunning, the brutal slaying of those whose number included his beloved Lars. There was a firm tugging within him demanding hatred. Why should not one hate evil men like these who had come upon them? Why should not one desire to' see revenge meted out with additional measure? Why should not— And then the Christlike glow returned.

Prest Gran went to his study... to pray for Bruno Schreckenbach!

Eight

PREST GRAN conducted his second mass funeral in a week, including the interment of his son.

Then he spent the next three days in bed.

The German attack continued throughout Norway. On Friday, April 12, the Germans, with three divisions of infantry, spread out from Oslo. One force moved to the south along the eastern shore of Oslo Fjord to brush aside the slight resistance from unorganized Norwegian groups; it passed through Bjerkely by night and was seen from darkened windows by eyes eager for gun sights. A second Nazi force moved to the northeast of Oslo. It met resistance at Skarnes, but was reinforced and drove the defenders to positions north of Kongsvinger. Still other forces spread, fan-like, to the northwest, west and southwest.

The Norwegian Government, which had begun evacuation from Oslo at the first news of the invasion, kept a hairsbreadth from the greedy Nazi clutches. The gold from the Bank of Norway in Oslo was safely evacuated with them. The old city of Hamar became the international center, where the personnel of the British Legation, the French Legation and the Polish Legation arrived by car. Here, also, was the new location for the American, Danish, and Dutch ministers, and the Belgian and Swedish *chargés d'affairs*.

On came the Nazi hordes, and when they were within ten miles of Hamar, this great company moved on to Elverum, a few miles northeast.

Vidkun Quisling, the Pro-Nazi Norwegian Iscariot, was not long in declaring himself Prime Minister, and his first order to the colonel commanding the Elverum District, one of his old comrades in the quest of betraying Norway, was: "I hold you personally responsible for the capture of the Royal Family, the Storting and the government."

With all of the fury launched on the Poles, the Germans bombed Elverum in a desperate effort to crush Norwegian resistance by striking at the core, the government, and King Haakon, whom the Norwegians loved with a patriotic fervor that would make Herr Hitler himself jealous.

Of Elverum's big buildings, only a church and a Red Cross hospital remained unscathed. Giant pillars, pointing accusing fingers at reconnaissance planes, were all that remained of some of the blasted buildings. Automobiles, left in the streets when their drivers ran for shelter, were blasted into pulp. Incendiary bombs burned the bark from trees, leaving them gaunt and charred, and sent melted snow down the gutters— where, too, might be seen a crimson stain suggesting human blood, though most of the eleven thousand population escaped death. It was not uncommon to see the Norwegian flag raised defiantly above bombed homes, where Nazi planes, flying so low that a bomb never missed its target (for there was no resistance) cast their shadows on the unfurled banners or increased their waving with the wind from the propellers.

But King Haakon showed no signs of softness from the years spent either in the luxurious Royal Palace during the summer, or at his simple summer residence a few miles away in Bygdoy, for, dressed in winter clothes, heavy boots, a thick topcoat, cap and ear muffs, both he and Crown Prince Olav escaped uninjured beneath the shelter of trees.

Trondheim, in the shelter of Trondheim Fjord, was captured by the German Navy and became a strategic spearhead. German guns were installed. The Agdenes fort was put into action, making it necessary for the British warships—had they dared attempt entrance to Trondheim harbor—to make two slow right-angle turns in the fjord bringing them point-blank into range of the fort guns.

On April 19 the British landed troops at Andalsnes, up the coast from Bergen. From here their troops launched attacks eastward past Dombas, to meet German troops coming westward from Lillehammer, and northward to Storen for another advance eastward and contact with the enemy in the Osterdal mountain ranges near Roros.

Yet another Allied attack began from the coast at Namsos, but it was of little consequence.

In the bosom of those majestic mountains which flank Andalsnes, the British unloaded their invasion equipment. They were contested by two flights of German bombers, kept high by those three thousand-foot peaks that hem in the Romsdalsfjord. But though only a tiny port, and thus inadequate for a full-sized invasion force (for Andalsnes' population was less than one thousand souls) the British made good their venture.

Up the mountain sides, down into the snow-caked valleys, over precarious peaks, across frozen waterways, advanced the British and Norwegian forces. They met the enemy at rocky heights where only men and mules, not armored divisions, can battle. Their gallant troop movements were consistently harried by German bombers that roared down between the mountain walls.

Norwegians blew up German transportation buses, most of which had been seized from the Norwegians. Around Oslo some of the bus drivers carved niches for themselves in history. The German officials had commandeered the big buses that run in every direction from the capital and forced the drivers to take Nazi soldiers to the various fronts for contact with the Allied forces. But some of the drivers, determined to put a stop to this, plotted among themselves, and one day three of the great buses being driven from Oslo to Honefoss went over the precipice near Solihogda, and sixty men in each bus, besides the driver, were killed.

The Nazis succeeded in driving all Allied organized resistance out of southern Norway, and the King, the Crown Prince and the government moved north with them, in the hope of driving the Germans farther and farther south. It was a great disillusion for the

Norwegian populace, but in a proclamation, the King declared that the northern movement was done in an effort to cope with the murderous Nazis, and the people remained optimistic. And this optimism was reflected in speeches delivered by the King and the Crown Prince over the Bodo radio station May 17, the national day of Norway.

But even before the optimistic proclamation, the real issue was settled, and the Nazis, in control of strategic Oslo and Trondheim, had things in hand. German troops occupied more and more of the cities and towns, and when their ranks goose-stepped down the streets, indignant Norwegians would turn their backs. Although German was taught in virtually all Norwegian schools, Norwegians suddenly were unable to understand or speak a word of German.

At last the King sought refuge in Sweden, and when it was certain that the Germans were successful in their invasion attempt and that his life was endangered each moment he remained on European soil, King Haakon accepted the invitation of the President of the United States and came to America.

It was a beautiful May morning in Bjerkely, and news was about that, although it was only six hours since Hitler had pledged that he would not harm his small lowland neighbors, the Nazi blitzkrieg was spreading death and terror into Holland, Luxembourg and Belgium.

Bruno Schreckenbach, radiant with joy, watched as a sign was posted in the town square.

It read:

> NOTICE! ALL MEN, NOR OTHERWISE EMPLOYED, ABOVE
> THE AGE OF NINETEEN AND BELOW THE AGE OR
> SIXTY-FIVE REPORT IN THE TOWN SQUARE AT ONE
> O'CLOCK TODAY

And as the tacks were being driven into the paper, trucks, driven by armed Germans, were roaring into town, laden with steel girders, cement sacks, and other construction equipment.

When he returned from town, Bjarne told Prest Gran of the developments.

"I guess," the minister smiled, "that verifies our assumption that the Germans have plans for Bjerkely."

"And to think that we are supposed to do the work... according to that order Schreckenbach had posted. There'll be trouble, won't there?"

"I think we've learned the lesson, Bjarne, that it is useless to fight back until we are prepared to do it. I wish it were possible to get people to see that."

"If I know the men of Bjerkely, they aren't going to like the idea of working for the Nazis, and some of them are stubborn enough to balk."

Prest Gran shook his head.

"The best strategy," Bjarne said, "is to let the Nazis go ahead, act like we're willing to be subjected, and then watch for a chance to strike back."

"It's difficult to know what to do... when the enemy is so ruthless. Now their fury is spreading into Western Europe. I wonder . . ." Prest Gran tried to seem brave, ". . . if they will continue until France and Great Britain, too, are conquered, and EurOpe is hopelessly lost for—"

"No!" Bjarne opposed. "That can't be!"

"It doesn't seem that God would allow it, but—"

"If only we could do something! For weeks, now, we've been sitting here, doing nothing, while Schreckenbach and his men have taken control of everything! I tell you, I can't stand it much longer!"

Sigurd stormed in.

"Work for the Nazis! Nothing doing!"

"You've heard the news, too?" Bjarne laughed a bit.

"If I ever pound a nail for a Nazi, it'll be on the lid of his rough box!"

"You're employed," Bjarne reminded, "aren't you? You're *dreng* here at the *Prestegaarden*."

"For that matter," Prest Gran chuckled, "Schreckenbach is so tired of your puns on him that he probably wouldn't hire you to —"

"Schreckenbach hasn't anything to do with whatever work's to be done here," Sigurd interrupted. "A Nazi big shot has come to town with all that equipment.

He's supposed to be a construction engineer, and he'll do all the hiring and bossing."

"I wonder what's to be built here," Bjame said. "It couldn't be an airport, and—"

Sigurd cut him off with, "Airport? Not much! There are surveyors down at the docks right now!"

"Is that true, Sigurd?"

"Sure it's true! I saw them myself! Schreckenbach has released that order that no one is to go near the fjord."

"Hm," Bjarne mused, "must be something brewing down there, then."

"I was right," Sigurd boasted.

"You certainly were," Prest Gran fueled his pride.

Bjarne said, "Schreckenbach's been unusually decent lately, hasn't he? Of course, there haven't been any uprisings, and so he hasn't had to be strict. He's been trying to get in with the men about town."

Sigurd chirped, "That's like trying to keep lions and tigers in one cage!"

"I don't know about that," Bjarne added. "I came to the hotel yesterday, and Schreckenbach and Leif Hunseid were having a friendly chat. If Leif Hunseid acts friendly toward Schreckenbach, it's not hard to believe that others might, too."

"Hunseid hates the ground Schreckenbach walks on, I thought," Sigurd said.

Bjarne assured, "Of course he does. He was a little flustered when I came on him and Schreckenbach, but I winked, to let Leif know I understood. I guess he's playing up to Schreckenbach so he can strike hard when the opportunity comes."

"I've been pleased at Leif Hunseid's attitude lately," Prest Gran said. "He's always been a regular church attendant, but when I question him, I can't get any definite statement of faith in Christ from him. I doubt if he's been born again. But 'he seems to be more responsive to the Gospel. I have hopes for him. Last . Sunday, when I spoke on faith under fire, he seemed to be deeply moved."

"Who wouldn't be," Bjarne emphasized, "the way you've been feeding the people's faith at the preaching services!"

Prest Gran smiled and said, "Perhaps this is a splendid opportunity for the preaching of the Gospel. If so,it's worth the hardship. You'll excuse me, please, gentlemen. It's Thursday, and'I have a great deal of work to do yet on my Sunday messages."

And so they went their various ways.

The town square was alive with men at one o'clock. Some were mumbling that they had not wanted to come but that their wives sent them. Others ventured that there was little use in balking until the right opportunity for resistance came. And others seemed only there out of curiosity.

Bruno Schreckenbach and a stranger came to the square.

"It is good to see you here, men," Schreckenbach began. "We appreciate your cooperation, and we assure you that it shall be rewarded. N ow that we have been successful in driving the British from Norway and are well on our way toward striking them on their home soil, perhaps you are beginning to realize that the Germans really are your friends and that we are here to help you."

He stopped for applause, though he hardly expected any... and his expectations were correct.

"A distinguished visitor has come to Bjerkely today. He is Hans Laub, eminent engineer from my beloved fatherland. He shall make his headquarters here for the next few weeks, and I shall ask him now to tell you his purpose in coming."

Hans Laub was in civilian clothes, but a swastika, on a white background, brought attention to his left arm. His fat face had the demanding characteristics of the executive—but it had also the fearless countenance of an executioner; and looking at the nervous gestures of his hands, one would wonder if they had ever graSped a cat-of-nine-tails, or thrown the switch to an electric chair, or pulled the lever that drops the trap door beneath a noose. The heavy mustache beneath his thick nose gave his teeth the appearance of fangs. His eyes were like two hot coals in the hands of a fiend eager to commit arson. His voice had the guttural resonance of a wild beast.

This was Hans Laub, whom Bjerkely was to, learn to know.

"Heil Hitler!" he saluted, before beginning his instructions. "I am here for business, important business. My esteemed government, the Third Reich, has chosen your town and given it the great privilege of serving in the job of making this world fit for living. I congratulate you.

"My good friend, Herr Schreckenbach, has done laudable work in bringing Bjerkely into subjection. Not one citizen has left the town limits, and the vigil of sentries is being increased, so that no one shall leave in the future.

"Bjerkely, with its deep-water fishing docks and its secluded location, has appealed to advance Nazi agents as an ideal location for a submarine base in the conflict against the Allied navies." A gasp from the crowd caused him to pause. "There is, then, much to be done. Loading docks must be constructed, dry docks erected, and, fortifications installed.

"This is a noble work!" he stormed, growing eloquent. "It is a humanitarian service! Bjerkely has a commission from justice! The world is being locked in the tentacles of a monster... a monster whose hunger is capitalism and whose food is wealth! The Nazi powers, ordained of God, are pledged to break this lethal grip! And that pledge shall be kept, finding fulfillment in the morning of victory! Heil Hitler!"

Now he called, after a pause. "Work begins at seven o'clock tomorrow morning. There will be but one shift, as we can't risk work at night. The Reich, fair in all its dealing, has asked that I pay the highest wages possible. Fifty *öre* an hour will be the minimum. Some will earn one krone an hour. Others will earn more. And initiative will be well rewarded," his eyes glared, "depending, of course, on the nature of that initiative.

"That's all. Report at the fishing docks tomorrow morning. Any who do not come will be chastised by the agents of the Gestapo stationed here!"

There was no applause. There were no smiles of approval. The men dispersed as silently as fog lifts from the *bakke*. A few were whispering, like the breeze that breaks the stillness of the fog. But that was all.

Nine

WORK AT THE FISHING DOCKS proceeded rapidly, and when the first week had passed, tons of concrete had been poured, and steel girders protruded from the fjord water like the fins of a school of sharks. News was abundant, too, of the constantly retreating Allied armies, and the onrushing Nazi mechanized forces, in the lowlands and against France.

Schreckenbach and Hans Laub were elated.

Standing on a construction platform, Laub called to the men at the close of the day's work, "A week has passed, men. Your hours have been recorded through Saturday night, and you will be paid up to that time. A week from today, your envelopes will cover an entire week's work."

Two armed Gestapo officers appeared, one carrying a steel box, and Laub continued, "Get in line, men! Show your identification cards, and your pay envelopes will be given to you."

Bjarne placed his envelope in his pocket and proceeded alone toward the *Prestegaarden*.

The evening air Was fragrant with the zest of summer, but it was winter in his heart. He was like a ship frozen in the arctic clutches of the Gulf of Bothnia. He was helping the enemy, but he did not want to. He should be thwarting the enemy's plans, but he could not.

The wintry blasts of defeat blew against his heart.

Borghild greeted him.

"Tired?" she asked.

He answered with the pressure of an emerging breath.

"Twelve hours a day is a long time," she said. "It's a wonder Laub doesn't demand work from sunup to sunset. But," she added, "you men have been promised time-and-a-half for overtime, figuring ten hours a day."

"It isn't the work that makes me tired," he sighed, dropping into a chair. "It's knowing that every pound of concrete that is poured, every rivet that's fastened, everything that's done is aiding Germany and hurting the Allies."

"But maybe you can strike, when the submarine base is completed."

"How? We haven't a thing to use for sabotage. Those Gestapo officers stand over us all day. We couldn't get by with anything. And they'll be just as vigilant when the construction is done."

"It's terrible, Bjarne, but..." And that was the end of her optimistic words, for she had nothing to follow the conjunction.

Sigurd came in from his evening chores.

"Hello, Bjarne! How do you like working for Hitler by now?"

"Bad joke, Sigurd," Bjarne scowled.

"Sure, I know," said Sigurd, softening. "I look at it this way. Help the little boy pile his blocks, and then when they're all piled," he winked, "good and high, knock them all down with one blow!"

"I hope we can gum this mess some way," Bjarne said, "but I don't know how."

"Don't you worry," Sigurd assured. "There'll be a way!" Then he asked, "You haven't seen any ships yet, have you... any submarines?"

Bjarne shook his head.

Sigurd laughed, "Maybe they're so camouflaged you can't see them. I heard about one Nazi shipbuilder who was so ambitious in his camouflaging he painted a life-size whale on the side of a warship... a whale spouting water!"

Bjarne chuckled in an undertone.

"I heard it was pay day today."

"That's right, Sigurd."

Borghild aSked, "How much have you earned, Bjarne?"

"I don't know. I haven't opened the envelope yet." As he spoke, he tore the end of the envelope and some paper currency emerged.

As he did, Sigurd said, "Can't be much NorWegian money around. The gold was moved from Oslo to Molde, and from there to Tromso. It was put on ship there—boy, are the Nazis mad!—and shipped to Canada. I heard there wasn't a marine or a soldier to guard it, but every ounce got across safe. The bullion was in barrels, roped together and put on deck with fixings that would make them float if the ship went down. But none of the gold ships —"

"Say," Bjarne interrupted, "what is this?"

Borghild asked, "What's the matter?"

"What kind of money is this?" he asked, holding it up to Borghild.

"It isn't Norwegian money," she said. From one of the bills, she read, "Reich's Credit Bank Voucher."

"Sounds fishy to me!" Bjarne said.

"Maybe," Sigurd suggested, "it's about as valuable as that inflation mark." His chuckle announced another joke. "I heard of a German peasant who hadn't paid for a farm he bought before the last war. He was so poor he only had two geese. He took them to market, and at inflation prices, they brought enough marks to pay off the mortgage on his farm. The fellow he paid the money to ran to the store, but by the time he got there bread had gone up so high it took all he got from the farm to buy a small loaf. Well, these Nazis—"

"You know," Bjarne interrupted, "I think that crook Laub has these printed right here in Bjerkely."

Borghild asked, "What makes you think that?"

"There's a big truck pulled up by his headquarters. I thought it was a printing press of some sort, that maybe he's getting out literature to spread propaganda, but he must be printing money. No wonder he pays me a *krone* and twenty-five *öre* an hour!"

"How terrible, Bjarne!"

"That's Nazis for you!" Sigurd chimed.

"There'll be trouble for Laub, if he tries much of this."

"And more trouble for Bjerkely," Borghild shivered.

"Well," Bjarne yawned, "I'm going to clean up a bit before supper."

"Birgit's visiting this afternoon, Bjarne," Borghild said, "so supper will be a little late."

"Good! I'll take a nap, too, then."

Alone, Borghild wandered outside. She paused in the garden to examine some bulbs which were sending their shoots above the ground, and she checked the growth of a cluster of buds, wondering how many days it would be until they bloomed. Beside the red wooden barn, imposing on its stone foundation, she stopped to run her fingers through the wool of a pet sheep. A calf came to her, sniffing inquisitively, but when she offered to pet it, it kicked lusty hind heels in the air, and with an alarmed baa, galloped into the barn to its mother.

And then, in another few moments, her pretty hand was a trolley on the top railing of the cemetery fence.

She stopped, for she could not walk and suppress the tears welling behind her eyes at the same time.

And then she continued, into the cemetery.

The new graves had been leveled, but they stood out in contrast to the grass, and the graves covered with bushes or flowers. She thought of that day when the Nazi plane had added to the enemy's toll. A bee idled by, and for a moment she feared she heard the roar of a plane.

At the graves of Lars and her mother, side by side, she stopped. She knelt. But the emotional storm that had been surging through her calmed. Instead of tears came smiles.

"Dear Mother and Lars," she whispered, "you are so happy... absent from the body, present with the Lord!"

She ran her fingers through the dirt on Lars' grave, as though stroking his hair, and pulled a small weed from her mother's grave, just as she had so often relieved her of cares while she was alive.

"Dear Mother and Lars! Dear Mother and Lars!"

A throat was cleared behind her. It startled her.

"Mr. Schreckenbach!" she gasped, standing.

"I'm sorry if I frightened you," he smiled. "I usually take a walk after my evening meal, and tonight I chose the restful dignity of the cemetery."

Her first impulse was to run; but it was the second impulse which she obeyed, the urge to shout, "Are you counting the graves you've contributed here?"

"Miss Gran!" he said. "I regret every grave here, just as much as you do! Tell me," again he smiled, "is that the grave of your mother?"

"Yes. And this is Lars' grave, Lars who was brutally_"

"Don't! Please don't, Miss Gran! That hurts me!"

"Hurts you?"

"It nearly killed me when that happened! I—"

"You lie! You lie! You aren't—"

"Believe me, Miss Gran! I was not to blame for those deaths!" He pleaded, "Believe me!"

With bold gestures of her eyes, she said, "When I think of what the future may hold, I am not sorry for Lars."

"The future will be bright, as soon as Germany has made the world safe from the—"

"Safe? Are your plundering armies making Holland safe, and Belgium, and—"

"You do not understand—"

"I understand what it must mean to have women and children, refugees, machine-gunned like—"

"You have been. listening to the radio, Miss Gran? Why don't you listen to the Berlin reports?"

"Because—"

"It is true," he interrupted, "that civilians have had to be attacked... but that has only been when their stubborn refusal to leave the highways has blocked the advance of our mechanized units. But let's not talk about the unfortunate things of war. Tell me, are you an admirer of Henrik Ibsen? I read his Hedda Gabler last night before I retired. I thought Mrs. Tesman and Eilert Lovborg were—"

"Ibsen was a great Norwegian," Borghild interrupted, but in a tone that indicated her disinterest.

"I strolled through the birch-shaded cemetery near Our Saviour's Church one afternoon when I was in Oslo. It impressed me that on the marble shaft and slab above Ibsen's grave there is no inscription, because none is needed. His works are the only epitaph he needs." He chuckled. "I have a liking for cemetery strolls, I guess. I visited the grave of Bjornson, too, and when I was in Bergen—"

"I must go, Mr. Schreckenbach. Good evening."

"Must you really? I love to talk, and you have impressed me as one who would make a good conversationalist."

"I—"

"What interests you most? Literature? I've read Bojer's The Last of the Vikings and Undeset's—"

"I don't care to—"

"Music? I know German critics who enjoyed Grieg more than Brahms or—"

"I'm sorry, Mr. Schreckenbach, but I must go!"

He asked softly, "Is-it because you must go, or is it because I am here?"

She didn't answer.

"Miss Gran, why can't I win the friendship of people like you?"

She started to laugh.

But he broke in with, "I'm serious. I am here for the good of Norway. Oh, I know you don't believe that, but you will. There have been mishaps, I know. Those five young men were killed, but if you would be fair, you will admit that it wasn't my fault; I warned them, but they deliberately broke my command—a command which, in time of war, is entirely legitimate. And... and the death, of your brother... Surely you don't believe that I—"

"Mr. Schreckenbach! How can you be such a fool? How can you deliberately—?"

"Miss Gran! _Please don't be so quick to form opinions! I—"

"Opinions? If you were going about your affairs peacefully, as we Norwegians were, and some fiends came and began murdering you and your people, your opiniOn would be—"

"Miss Gran!"

"Oh, I think you're horrible! I detest the sight of you, and of every German in Bjerkely! I think you're vile, everyone of you! I think Hans Laub is a thief— making our men work like slaves and then paying them worthless paper!" This caused Schreckenbach to lurch, but she didn't give him time to speak. "I would rather be dead than be known as a friend of any of you! You're murderers! You're thieves! You're brutal, selfish, vulgar! You—" But here her tongue stopped, like an engine so hot that its pistons have been warped and locked in the cylinders.

Bruno Schreckenbach did not offer further argument. He seemed hurt, defenseless, and his arms hung limply at his side as he stared at her. Twice his lips moved, but his silence was not broken. He dropped his eyes a moment, then returned them to again gaze at her. Once more his lips moved, but there were no words. He swallowed hard, turned and, walked away.

Borghild felt a strain of pity leave her heart, but when it was shared about her furious body, it lost its potency and she was glad for everything she had said.

Far down a row of tombstones, she saw Bruno Schreckenbach stop his mournful pace, turn like a stiff old man, and once more look at her. From this more distant view, he was almost handsome —tall, rugged, youthful. But he seemed so forsaken, like an orphan unclaimed by his rightful parents and unwanted by others.

Perhaps there were good things about him. Perhaps beneath that outer crust of Nazi fanaticism was fertile soil which, if cultivated by right relationships, would keep his life from going to weeds. Perhaps he had, beneath his Gestapo airs, the abilities to love, to take a woman for his own and be a companion whose constant quest would be toward increasing her happiness. Perhaps he loved the good things of life, in spite of his discipleship to Nazism. Perhaps—

Yes, she was sorry for him, very sorry. But there was nothing she could do to help him.

She turned and hurried home.

Bruno Schreckenbach watched every step she took; and it was dark before he left his vigil—a hope that she would step outside her door so he could see her again before returning to the hotel.

Ten

THE MEN WERE SULLEN at work the next day, and everywhere were words like these:

"Occupation money! It's worthless!"

"If you tried to exchange this in Germany, you'd be laughed at!"

"We're working for nothing... that's what we're doing!"

The concrete pouring decreased fifty per cent in momentum. Sturdy men—who had skimmed through the woods on skis, carrying a bowl of liquid, and had made figure eights without spilling a drop—stumbled over mere shadows and dropped their loads of cement sacks... usually near the water so that large quantities could be wasted. One concrete mold was Constructed with weak supports, and when the pouring was begun, several tons of carefully mixed concrete oozed into the fjord.

"Blockheads!" Hans Laub cursed. "Cement is rationed to us! Who built that cement form?"

But no one answered him, for all the carpenters were Norwegians, and none of them had ever cast his vote for Quisling.

"Who built that cement form?" Hans Laub repeated. "I demand an answer!"

But there was no answer.

"Do you know what the Reich does with saboteurs?"

No one answered.

Hans Laub stiffened with anger, and, in words that might have passed as thunder if they had not been articulate, shouted, "If one more boner is pulled, there will be no pay to anyone for the week's work! Do you hear me? Unless everything runs smooth, no pay for one week! Must you learn the hard way, swine?" He waved his arm defiantly, "Get to work, all of you!"

A brawny middle-aged mason, whose biceps had been forged by manual labor in the mighty Rjukan nitrogen works in Telemark Province, dropped his trowel. He moved toward Laub, bold as a marten attacking a larger prey.

"What would it matter," he blared, "if we didn't get paid? Do you think we're children? Toy money!"

"What are you talking about, swine?" Hans Laub demanded. "Aren't you satisfied with—?"

"You pay us toy money!" the Norwegian interrupted.

"Toy money?"

The mason held up one of the bills that had come in his pay envelope. Tearing it to bits, he defied, "It's worthless!"

"Fool!" Laub shouted. "Don't tear up good money! Haven't you any sense of value?"

"You talk about values! Why don't you pay us good Norwegian money?"

"Do you think! we're bank robbers, idiot? How can—?"

"What good is this?" the workman demanded.

"The stores will honor it! I have demanded that!"

"And what do the stores use to restock their shelves?"

"Get to work, swine!"

"And if we can buy with this trash," he tore another bill, "what do we do with the surplus..." he sneered, "save it?"

"Get to work!" Hans Laub repeated. "You are wasting time!" Shaking a fist at the onlookers, he shouted, "You, too! Get to work! This isn't a playground!"

"We'll work," the Norwegian continued his defiance, "when you pay us in Norwegian currency!"

Hans Laub shrieked, "Do you make demands of the Reich, swine?"

"I demand that—"

"Quiet! Get busy or I'll have you shot!"

"You don't—"

"Busy, I said! Fool! You're as blockheaded as a Pole, as a Frenchman, a Britisher, a Jew! Don't you know men die for daring to contest the program of our Führer?"

The working area covered one hundred yards of shoreline, and there were two men for every yard, though spread from one extreme of the project to the other. All attention on the water front was given to Hans Laub and the man who had put into action the defiant wishes of all. Some gripped their shovels, and tried to believe that they had possession of guns. Some nudged heavy rocks with their toes, seriously considering the use of a weapon so crude. Others nodded their heads, and Laub did not know which of the two they were supporting. Others stood aghast, and nothing more.

The bold Norwegian mason advanced another step toward Hans Laub, so close that when the Nazi swung his fist, demanding, "Get to work or I'll have you shot!" the distance between the fist and the chin was narrow. And then that distance ceased to exist, though it was now the Norwegian's fist which made a deep thud on the mouth of the engineer!

There was a surging rumble of mingled sounds from the men.

Hans Laub fell back, but he kept his balance. The Norwegian continued his advance, his fist loaded and aimed at its retreating target.

"Stop, swine!" Hans Laub bellowed. "Don't come near me!"

But the Norwegian came, a step behind Laub's backward movement.

When the Nazi was backed against a concrete mixer, flanked on one side by gravel and on the other by cement sacks, he cried, "Stop, I say! Bruno, where are you? Bruno! Tell your men to shoot!"

Bruno Schreckenbach was not on the scene, but a half dozen of his Gestapo men were. And from the position of one came the ghastly bark of a Krupp rifle. The Norwegian slumped at the feet of Hans Laub.

The Norwegian was dead!

"Good work!" Laub" exclaimed, shrieking with delight. "Good shot, man, good work!"

And then all was silent on the water front, so silent that the waves seemed to be treading carpets of_ seaweed, and the wind blowing only where it would make no sound.

It was Hans Laub who made the first sound. "There! That is what happens to fools! Do you see? That is what happens to fools!"

Then it was as silently silent as before.

"You!" Hans Laub pointed to a young fellow in his last teens.

The youth swallowed and stared.

"I said you! Come here!"

The youth came.

Hans Laub sneered, "Pick up the carcass of this rebel!"

The youth tenderly lifted the limp form of his comrade. All could now see that he had been shot through the head.

Pointing to a mold half filled with concrete, Hans Laub demanded, "Take him over there!"

The youth seemed bewildered.

"I said, take him over there! Idiot! Swine!"

The youth was more bewildered.

"Follow me!" Hans Laub shouted. "A dog knows enough to do that!"

The youth followed Hans Laub. In his arms he had the dead mason.

Beside the half filled mold, the Nazi stopped, and pointing at the moist concrete, said, with a sneer, "That is his grave."

The youth did not understand.

"I said that is his grave!"

The youth's mouth opened, and he was trembling.

"Throw him in there!"

The youth clutched the body, rather than released it.

"Throw him in there! Are you a dunce? Don't you understand?"

The youth shied from the gaping hole.

"Idiot!" Hans Laub threatened. "If you don't obey me, I'll have you shot, too! Now throw him in there! ...Do you hear me? Throw him in there!"

The youth heard; but he did not obey.

"Throw him in there! You defiant fool, throw him in there!" In desperation, Hans Laub turned to the nearest Gestapo agent and demanded of him, "Shoot this young fool!"

The Gestapo agent obeyed.

It was a simple matter for Hans Laub to kick the two dead men into the concrete mold. He did not know that the comrades were father and son, and that rather than be separated, they would have it this way.

Turning to the other workers, Laub demanded, "Have you learned from observation, or must you, too, learn from experience?"

All were silent, like mourners, drained of tears, beside an open grave.

"You," the Nazi snapped, pointing at three men with wheelbarrows, "come here!"

The three obeyed.

"Pour your concrete on those two swine!"

The three hesitated.

"In the name of the Reich, I swear you shall meet the same fate if you don't obey me! Pour your concrete on those swine! Do you hear me? Pour your concrete on those two fools!"

Fearfully, the three Norwegians obeyed for, in their hearts, they were sure that the two dead men would have had it so.

"There!" Hans Laub beamed. "That is better! All right, the rest of you, get busy! You concrete mixers! Finish filling that mold... that tomb! Everybody, get to work!"

Numb fingers and dull minds went to work, and things proceeded so slowly that Hans Laub did not cool his temper for the remainder of the day.

Eleven

BJERKELY WENT ITS WAYS like a prisoner in shackles. The sentries had shot five boys for attempting to escape. Bruno Schreckenbach insisted that the machine gunning at the cemetery was accidental, but the shooting of the two workers had been brutally executed by Hans Laub as a warning to all in the town. Now Bjerkely knew fear.

May sped over the calendar steps. King Leopold surrendered the Belgian Army to prevent further bloodshed. And then came Dunkirk—the miracle of Dunkirk—whose story is unknown to none.

June came, bringing with it the clash of an alleged irrepressible force (the Nazi Army) against the impregnable Maginot Line. That, too, is a well-known story—though the conflict ended in less than two weeks, followed by the French-German treaty.

Italy, traitor to her former allies, had begun pro-German aggression.

Bjerkely, informed by Nazi bulletins (confirmed by British radio reports) of the German victories, became submissive to the despotic Hans Laub, and the Gestapo head, Bruno Schreckenbach.

What else was there to do?

There was one ray of hope. Winston Churchill had taken the office of Prime Minister. He said in the House of Commons: "The Battle of Britain is about to begin. On this battle depends the survival of Christian civilization... Hitler knows he will have to break us in this island or lose the war."

Bjerkely was hopeful... but fearful. For vast darkness can tend to dim the brightest ray of hope.

The concrete docks were finished. There was not much left to do until submarines would be using Bjerkely as a base for blasting any British advances into the North Sea.

Little wonder that Bjerkely's hopefulness was anemic.

It was late evening, and the midnight sun lighted Bjerkely... but cast fearful shadows in its trail— shadows of stooped women, who, a few months ago, had been straight; of weary men, not long since sprightly; of children, shunning secluded places, never playing, never laughing; and of Gestapo agents boldly bearing their guns... like cowards!

Prest Gran, at his study window, watched the shadows.

"Father." Borghild was at his door.

He turned to her, and she entered.

"Bjarne says they are through at the docks... the men from town. Germans are coming to install guns and finish other works."

Prest Gran sighed.

"Is there nothing we can do, Father? Is it right for us to sit here, doing nothing?"

Prest Gran sighed a second time.

"Is justice dead in the world, Father?"

Prest Gran sighed a third time. But this time he spoke. "Justice is inevitable, my dear, until the just God is dethroned. That is a task too great for Hitler, thank God!"

"But what will happen, Father? England is the last stronghold, and if the Germans bomb England as they have—oh, Father, what will happen? Will America help?"

"Perhaps." America is helping now. But... " "Too little and too late! Too little and too late! Is that our doom?"

"Borghild dear," Prest Gran said softly, placing a hand on each of his daughter's shoulders. "It is not well when we place our confidence in circumstances, rather than in the sure promises of God. He has promised, I will never leave thee, nor forsake thee. Weeping may endure for a night, but joy cometh in the morning. Let us put our confidence in promises like these!"

"I know it's not right to doubt, and to be fearful, but—"

"I understand, dear. I understand."

Borghild looked into the face of her father. It had aged these few weeks, more than she had noticed before. At first she was startled, but then she saw what had come with the change. Lines? Yes. 'And the exit of dark hairs on his head. But, like the mellowing age of a violin, his voice had found a new resonance—perhaps from a heart enlarged from bearing many burdens. And his senile face challenged the radiance of the sun, though his face cast no shadows, as did the sun.

"You are so wonderful, Father! What would I ever do without you?"

She looked up at him for a moment, then smiled her first smile of the day.

"Where's Bjarne?"

"Outside with Sigurd. Did you want him?"

"I thought I'd go up and see Leif Hunseid this evening."

"Something that—"

"He seems so dejected lately. I'm afraid Leif Hunseid hasn't his faith in Christ. For a time I had hopes, though he's always been a paradox, religiously irreligious. It is dangerous not to have faith in Christ... when all is so dark about us."

"Yes," Borghild agreed, for her faith was newly strengthened. "I'm sure Bjarne is outside somewhere." "I believe I'll get my hat and go out and find him."

Borghild was alone in the house, except for Birgit who was upstairs.

It was very quiet—the silence that invites solemn thought, not the silence that breeds fear.

She read her Bible in the light of the midnight sun.

> Finally, my brethren, be strong in the Lord, and in the power of his might.

> Put on the whole armor of God, that ye may be able to stand against the wiles of the devil.

For we wrestle not against flesh and blood, but against principalities, against powers, against the rulers of the darkness of this world, against spiritual wickedness in high places.

Wherefore take unto you the whole armor of God, that ye may be able to withstand in the evil day, and having done all, to stand.

Stand therefore, having your loins girt about with truth, and having on the breastplate of righteousness;

And your feet shod with the preparation of the gospel of peace;

Above all, taking the shield of faith, wherewith ye shall be able to quench all the fiery darts of the wicked.

And take the helmet of salvation, and the sword of the Spirit, which is the word of God.

That was the secret of her father's strength! This was why no discouragements had disarmed him of his faith!

As she quietly meditated, she determined that she, too, would be more confident in the protection of this armament! Again and again she read the inspired words; each time it was like increasing the thickness of the walls of a citadel.

Then she prayed. She prayed for Bjerkely—for her mothers, her fathers, her sons, her daughters, her bereaved ones, her perplexed ones, her doubting ones. She prayed for the ministry of her father. She prayed that God would bring peace, according to the perfect workings of His will.

It was not easy, but she prayed for their enemies—for German soldiers forced to kill against their better desires, for German pilots whose bombs had made childless mothers and motherless children, for Hans Laub... for Bruno Schreckenbach.

Sigurd entered, and she looked up.

"Hello," she greeted, smiling.

He chuckled, "It's good to see somebody smiling!"

"Why shouldn't I," she asked, holding her Bible to her heart, "when I have this?"

Sigurd gave his head a characteristic nod.

"These difficulties have been a blessing to me, Sigurd. They've taken me closer to God."

Again he nodded.

"German occupation is horrible, but if Christ occupies our hearts, the worst is wonderful!"

He changed the subject a bit, saying, "Might be bad by winter. Food is going to be rationed here in the next few days."

"Yes," she agreed, "it will, be hard. I've heard that the Nazis are rigidly rationing food in Belgium and France. The refugee conditions there must be horrible... so many have lost their homes, so many women and children have no means of support."

"Dirty Nazis!" Sigurd fumed.

"God will judge them!"

"It can't come soon enough to suit me!"

"I don't know how soon... but I am sure."

"I can keep good-natured, Borghild, if I have enough to eat, but if those Nazis start stealing food from us, like I hear they've done in the lowlands and France..." _He chuckled, the prelude to another of his jokes. "I heard on the radio that they have already made a decree in Belgium that the farmers can't feed grain to their chickens. The other day a Gestapo officer, who'd heard reports of fat chickens in his territory, checked up on the farmers. He came to one farm and found the chickens as fat as two-and-a-half-pound spring fries. 'What do you feed these fowls?' he asked the farmer, and the farmer had to admit it was oats. Off he went to a concentration camp. The chickens on the next farm were every bit as fat. 'What do you feed them?' the Nazi yelled, and then he saw oats, and another Belgian went to the concentration camp. The chickens on the third farm were fatter than at the other two places. 'What do you feed them?' the Gestapo agent asked this farmer, same's the others. 'Nothing,' replies the Belgian. 'What do you mean... nothing?' asks the Nazi. He searched the place, and he didn't find a single grain. 'What makes these chickens so fat, if you don't feed them any grain?' he demanded. 'Well,' said the Belgian," Sigurd's countenance warned of the climax, "'to the Nazi, it's simple. I have two thousand hens and only one rooster. I've named the rooster Adolf, and he takes the hens out to eat up all the neighbor's feed!'

Yes, sir, and I bet that rooster could crow! And like as not the hens cackled, Heil Hitler, every time they laid an egg!"

Borghild laughed, "I dare you to tell that to Schreckenbach or Hans Laub!"

"Just give me a chance!" Sigurd winked. "Just give me a chance!"

"If that's the way you feel about it," she smiled, "I withdraw my dare."

"Nothing about those fellows to make a man afraid. Put them on the other side of a gun once, and they'd wilt."

"Get them on the other side of the gun first, though, before you try anything. We've learned some hard lessons, you know."

"And we're going to put into good use everything we've learned! It'll be our turn one of these days!"

"And when it is," Borghild smiled, "we'll be fair, won't we? We'll have learned that in our lessons!"

"Maybe so," he mumbled. "Well, I've got a big day tomorrow. I'll be getting to my room. Good night, Borghild."

"Good night."

Again she gave attention to her Bible, musing through its pages like a fabulously rich princess who munches where she wishes from a bountiful banquet table.

The door chimes sounded.

Through the small window, Borghild saw that it was Bruno Schreckenbach. The door was locked. She would refuse him admittance. He rang again._ She knew he would continue ringing, and Sigurd or Birgit would come down. Why should she be afraid? Sigurd was upstairs.

She opened the door.

"Miss Gran," Bruno Schreckenbach bowed, "I didn't expect to be so graciously admitted."

"My father is not here," she said, standing in his way.

"I wanted to see him."

"He has gone to spend the evening with Leif Hunseid. You will find him there, if you care to—"

"Perhaps he will soon be back. I can wait for him."

"But—"

"Mr. Kolstad has gone, too?"

Before she could stop the words, they had said, "He is."

Schreckenbach brightened, and, inch by inch, came inside.

"You can find my father at Leif Hun—"

"I will wait," Schreckenbach said, drawing Borghild into the arms of his eyes.

She could feel their hot grasp.

She shrank from them.

He came closer.

There was nothing else to say but, "Will you sit down?"

"Thank you," he smiled, and went to the living room. "You will sit down, too?"

"I—"

She had planned to go upstairs and call Sigurd, but he insisted, "Please, Miss Gran. I think we can find interesting conversation." Again he smiled—if not the genuine, the corruption of an amiable smile—and chuckled, "I have been reading Ibsen, Undeset, Bojer and Lie since last we talked. Last night I read Peer Gynt and the night before, A Doll's House. What have you been reading lately?"

"The Bible," she said spontaneously.

"The...uh..."

The thought of the Book made her brave. She said, "You should read the Bible, Mr. Schreckenbach!"

"I have," he blurted, then slowly added, "many times."

She was surprised.

"It is one of the greatest—"

"The greatest, Mr. Schreckenbach! Jesus said, Heaven and earth shall pass away: but my words shall not pass away. His Word is eternal!"

Schreckenbach's eyes sought the floor.

And she was silent.

It was very silent in the house, like the footsteps of the shadows that fell across Bruno Schreckenbach and reached for her.

"I have wanted to come and see you before," he began.

"See me?" she startled. "But I thought you came to see—"

"I came to see you," he blushed. "When I saw your father and Mr. Kolstad go tonight, I knew at last I would find you—"

"Mr. Schreckenbach!" she flared. "You knew I was alone? Why did you lie, and say you came to see my father?"

"I...uh..."

"The Nazis specialize in lies!"

"You are clever," he stumbled, "as a lawyer of the People's Court."

"I'm not clever! But you're stupid!"

"Am I, Miss Gran? Am I stupid?"

He seemed hurt. And it always tempted her sympathies when anything was hurt, songbird or serpent. She was sorry.

"Perhaps I am," he said.

"What do you want to see me about, Mr. Schreckenbach?"

"What about?"

She nodded.

"About," he cleared his throat, "about... you."

"Me? Have I violated some—"

"Miss Gran," Bruno Schreckenbach interrupted, "I have waited many nights for this chance. I am busy during the day and sometimes at night, but whenever I had the opportunity, I have hidden in the brush beside the farm waiting for this chance. But I could never be sure of finding you alone... until tonight."

She slumped into a chair, too frightened to stand.

He, too, sat down.

"I want you for a friend, Miss Gran."

"F-Friend?"

"Yes."

"B-But—"

"Do you hate me?" he asked bluntly.

"I... the Bible teaches... I..."

"Do you hate me, Miss Gran?"

"N-No, but—"

"Do you dislike me very much?"

"You have been very unkind to our people."

"But I had to do that. You would think me a fool to betray my country, wouldn't you?"

"I can't—"

"Don't think of me as the Gestapo officer," he begged. He looked at her the way Bjarne did that romantic night when he had kissed her in the shadows of the university at Oslo. Then she was thrilled, but not now. He asked, "Can't you think of me tonight as Bruno Schreckenbach?"

Bruno Schreckenbach! That sounded more horrible than Gestapo!

"Please, Miss Gran?"

"I..."

"Why must we be such slaves to mere fancies? This war will be over in a few months. Germany will have proved its friendship to Norway. Then," he took a fortifying breath, "there will be no barriers. Germans will visit Norway; Norwegians will study in Germany... Norwegians and Germans will intermarry again, like the parents of Leif Hunseid, one of Bjerkely's most loyal citizens. I could wait until then, if—"

"Bruno Schreckenbach, what are you talking about?"

"About you, Miss Gran! About you! You are the most lovely person I have known! I am hypnotized by the thought of you! I thought women were no more than puppets these days, willing to stoop to any depth for the fancies of men... until I met you."

She stood, and held up her left hand where a diamond-studded ring sat upon its throne.

"Don't you know that Bjarne and I are—?"

He, too, stood.

"I knew, Miss Gran, and that is why I have been so hesitant to —"

"There are no Quislingers in true love!" she shouted, stomping her foot.

"I only—"

"You are a Nazi! You would steal a wife from her husband's arms, if she appealed to you! You would—"

"Miss Gran! Please! Please!"

"Isn't it true?"

"I would do that for only one woman... for you!"

His eyes were binoculars, enlarging for her the vast reaches of his heart.

"Mr. Schreckenbach," she gasped, "I—"

He stepped to her, took her hand. She was afraid, and, sick from that fear, could not free herself.

"Beautiful hand!" he exclaimed. He stooped and kissed it.

"Don't!" she begged.

He kissed it again.

With a desperate effort, she pulled it from his grasp.

"I love you, Miss Gran!"

"Don't say that!"

"It is true!"

He took her hand again, and she could not get away.

"Please!" she begged.

"Don't ask to get away, Miss Gran. I'm trying to win you, not enslave you. Believe me!"

She could not speak.

He held both of her hands now, and, searching her pale face, said, "I would betray the Führer... for you!"

"You have been betrayed—"

"Let's not stain moments like this with politics!"

"Mr. Schreckenbach," she freed one hand, "please go. I can't—"

"Your eyes give me hope, Miss Gran!... otherwise, I would go."

"No! No, they don't! I love my Bjarne, do you hear? I wouldn't betray him—"

"You betray yourself, unless you seek your own happiness. It is no sin to break—"

"Please go!" she screamed. "You can't stay any longer! You can't! Go! Please go!"

"It would be embarrassing if someone found us?"

"Go!" She pointed to the door. "Hurry!"

"Need help, Borghild?" It was Sigurd's voice from upstairs.

Bruno Schreckenbach clutched the handle of his gun; thus her other hand was also free.

"I'll go," he whispered. "I am busy tomorrow night, but the next night I will stroll in the cemetery. No one can see us there. Will you meet me, just at sunset?"

"Go!"

"Will you meet me, Miss Gran?"

"I said go!"

Sigurd's footsteps were heard.

"You will meet me," he said. "You will meet me in the cemetery. I am a gentleman. You needn't be afraid."

He left the house.

"What's wrong?" Sigurd asked. "I heard you were having trouble."

"It was Bruno Schreckenbach."

"Thought it was his voice. What did he want?"

"We... we," she searched her vocabulary, "argued."

"Good for you, girlie!" He patted her shoulder. "Let him know Bjerkely's against him... to the last one of us!"

"We're all against him," she said meekly.

"Sure we are! And we'll have them Nazis out of here before you know it." He whispered, and his eyes twinkled, "I've been studying night and day, almost, now that the project at the water front is about finished, for a way to break up the Nazi's plans. Would I like to see that water front get about a dozen bombs dropped into it!"

"We've got to do something, don't we?"

"Sure we do. Trouble is, we've got no way to get dynamite. If," he brightened, "we could get word to the R. A. F. some way, so's they could drop bombs— wouldn't that make the Nazis sing something instead of Erika, or whatever they call that song?—but," his enthusiasm waned, "there's no way to get news to England, so far as I can see."

"There must be some way," she said, still numb from the encounter with Schreckenbach.

"How? There hasn't been a letter sent out of Bjerkely. I've been kind of hoping that our relatives in Sweden and the like would take the hint and send British planes over, but," he sighed, "it's probably the same all over Norway, and nobody ever suspected that the Nazis planned to use Bjerkely for a submarine base."

"There must be some way," she said again.

"Maybe so, but I don't know what it is."

"There must be some way," she repeated a third time.

"Say! That Schreckenbach must have scared the life out of you! What's the matter?"

Sigurd surveyed the change in Borghild's eyes, the bleach upon her cheeks, the constant twitching about her lips.

"He didn't threaten you, did he?"

"N-No!"

"Listen," Sigurd pleaded, "if he's plotting anything, you're ahead to let us know about it, so we can—"

"It's nothing like that."

"You can trust—"

"Really, Sigurd!"

"Well," he frowned, "I guess looking at him is enough to scare some strong men. He'd be a good looking chap, if it weren't for that uniform and the swastika, I suppose, but as far as I'm concerned, he, and Laub, and the rest of the Nazis here make the poorest characters for a dream I can think of. What did he talk about?"

"We didn't agree."

"Must have been politics," Sigurd chuckled. "I'll be getting to bed. I suppose you're waiting to kiss Bjarne good night, or I'd tell you to get to bed, too."

"Yes," she said, "I'm waiting for Bjarne."

"Good night," he said, reclimbing the stairs.

"Good night, Sigurd."

"Don't be afraid! The Lord's watching over us!"

"I'm not afraid!"

Prest Gran and Bjarne had not hurried to the hotel, where Leif Hunseid had been forced to play host to the Nazis.

"Nature remains chaste," the minister mused, "whatever the vices of men."

"Just so no bombs fall on Bjerkely," Bjarne said.

"We'll hope not, or at least be optimistic until they do."

"If they'd fall in the submarine base," Bjarne whispered, "I—"

"Guard your lips, Bjarne! There are ears everywhere!"

Bjarne shuddered.

A hazel hen skimmed over the ground ahead of them. Prest Gran was an ardent spectator. When it was gone, a squirrel barked at them.

"Sounds something like Schreckenbach, doesn't he?" Bjarne joked.

They walked on.

At the hotel, Bjarne said, "We'll have to ring. Hunseid has been given orders to keep locked—wait a minute! The latch is on, but whoever entered last didn't close the door so it could catch."

"We had better ring anyway."

"That's no use. Leif's room is on the main floor. If he isn't in, we'll slip out again." Slowly opening the door, Bjarne whispered, "I wouldn't like for one of Laub's pet sentries to come to the door, especially if he hadn't had a good shot for a few days, which, thank God, none of them has."

"Shouldn't we ring?"

"No," Bjarne said, pushing the minister ahead of him.

Prest Gran whispered, "I haven't been in here since the invasion."

"I, either."

The swastika was prominent in the lobby. The Norwegian flag was gone. Of course, that was to be expected.

On the clerk's desk lay two Skoda guns.

"Look," Bjarne whispered.

"I see."

"Shall... I take them?"

"No, Bjarne!"

"But—"

"What could two guns do? They would be missed, and there would be trouble. And if you used them... No, Bjarne!"

"You are right," Bjarne agreed. "I won't take them."

"Thank you."

"Listen. Sounds like Leif has company."

"That does seem to be coming from his room."

Giving full attention, they heard:

"Yes sir, Laub, we've got Bjerkely at our finger tips."

"The work has been well done," Laub's voice, "and I am entirely satisfied. In another week or two, our submarines will be advancing against the British from the base."

"And nobody suspects me, Laub! Sly work, don't you think?"

"Very clever," Hans Laub agreed.

Bjarne's thick tongue managed to whisper, "I-Isn't that Leif Hunseid talking to Laub?"

"Can't be, Bjarne."

They moved cautiously closer to the origin of the voices.

From inside came, "Yes, Hunseid, you Quislingers can be proud of your work! I wish we had the foothold in England that we had here in Norway when we invaded."

It was Leif Hunseid! And he laughed, as he said, "The Britons have learned a lesson from 'the gentle Scandinavians! They are on the alert for Trojan horse activity!"

"Oh, well, our *Luftwaffe* will make quick work of those islands before long. I understand Goering has been making plans ever since the fall of France." Hans Laub hastily added, "You will keep that confidential, of course!"

"Do you think I'm a traitor?" Leif Hunseid asked, with abundant satire.

Hans Laub laughed.

Leif Hunseid laughed, too.

"Yes," Leif Hunseid continued, "I've even made old man Prest Gran think I was getting religious, I believe!"

Hans Laub laughed again.

Leif Hunseid laughed again, too.

"Let us go, Bjarne," the Prest whispered.

But Bjarne stood, and as Prest Gran sought to lead him, he felt the surgings of his muscles, the impatient twitching of every nerve.

"You know, Leif," Hans Laub continued, "if the British knew how important this little fishing town nestled here in the hills is, they'd send every plane they've got over here."

"If they knew," Leif Hunseid chuckled.

"That is why we will win the war, Leif, because we are so clever. It takes power to win wars, but a midget, with brains, can harness a dumb horse. We have done things cleverly, Leif, very cleverly! This great accomplishment at Bjerkely is only an example. I was at Wirtheim a few months before I came to Norway. They have built hangars in the country there which are underground. And their doors are camouflaged into the hillsides. The staffs live in farmhouses above ground, the weather and radio crews have their laboratories in the stock barns, and the Windmill is a beacon. There are seventy-five planes in each of those hangars. Isn't that clever, Leif?"

Leif must have nodded.

Hans Laub continued, "At dawn every morning, Heinkels came out of those hiding places and bombed the lowlands." He sneered, "They'll be over London soon!"

"Sure they will!" Leif Hunseid agreed.

"We are ready for the lethal attack. It won't take long. I tell you, Leif, the way of the conqueror suits me!"

"Me, too!" the Quislinger echoed.

"But getting back to Bjerkely, the British would never expect a submarine base here. You see, it's only two hundred and eighty miles from Stavanger to England, but the British would have spied on us before we'd have done a week's work along there. They'll never expect anything in Oslo Fjord!"

"How soon will we have U-boats in our water, Hans?"

"Perhaps days, Leif! Perhaps only days!"

"Good!"

"You know, I've always been in favor of the submarine. I didn't know a lot about them before the last war, but I remember that even then I didn't quite agree with Admiral Alfred von Tirpitz when he opposed adding submarines to the fleet." He laughed, "But German submarines rule the seas, Leif! Remember back in 1916? The Deutschland, one of our first Uboats, went to the United States carrying merchandise." He renewed his laugh, "The next year, as the U-155, _ she went into United States waters again... as a raider!"

"I saw the U—ZO," Hunseid said, "the submarine that sank the Lusitania, after it had gone aground in Denmark in... let's see... I believe it was November of 1916."

"I remember that boat! The crew blew a hole in her bow before abandoning her, didn't they?"

"That's right. I remember that now."

"With submarines, Leif, we can help the *Luftwaffe* finish their job in a short time! If Churchill would tell his people how many tons our U-boats have sent to the bottom, they'd beg him to surrender!" He paused a moment. "We've always got the menace of the hydrophone, the depth charge and the trailer bag, but, for that matter, the *Luftwaffe* doesn't expect to be immune from antiaircraft batteries and fighter planes.

"You know, Leif, there's a funny story connected to this depth-charge campaign by the British Navy. Whenever a U-boat is struck, a film of oil comes to the surface." His laughter again. "Our U-boats have been playing possum with the British. They squirt oil to the surface, when a depth charge misses its mark, and the British, proud as peacocks, chalk up another direct hit, while the submarine goes on its way unharmed!

"Yes, Leif, Bjerkely is bound for Nazi fame. I wouldn't be surprised if boats like the U-35 would be coming our way in a few weeks."

"It's going to make me proud!" Hunseid thrilled. "I've been waiting years for this!"

"You've done a mammoth job, Leif! Herr Hitler himself has spoken your name as an example of loyalty! He has spoken it only to the intimacy of the Reichstag, of course, but some day Germany will bestow the well earned praise on heroes like you!"

"I have been glad to do my part, Hans."

"You are a faithful Nazi, Leif! It is men like you who have given Nazism its European foothold!"

Prest Gran dragged Bjarne down the carpeted corridor, through the lobby, and to the door.

"I can't believe it," Bjarne muttered.

"Come, before we are seen."

"I'll shut the door, so Laub and Leif will never suspect that they might have been heard."

"Yes, Bjarne, shut the door."

They sought the darkest places homeward. Once, near the outskirts of town, they passed a sentry. Prest Gran greeted the man cheerfully.

With one foot on the soil of the *Prestegaarden*, Bjarne said, "Prest Gran, I've got to beat Hunseid within a hairsbreadth of—"

"No, Bjarne!"

"But—"

"No one can be more deeply hurt than I."

"Then why can't—"

"Don't you think it is best that only you and I know of Leif's treachery, Bjarne?"

"Well..."

"You see, it would only mean trouble. We must avoid trouble, whenever possible. There have been no deaths since that afternoon at the fjord. I pray it will be long until there will be any more."

"How can I look that traitor in the face, Prest Gran, and not give him the punishment he deserves?"

"He will get his punishment, Bjarne! Let God be both judge and giver of judgment. He will do it fairly! If we keep this to ourselves, we can watch Leif more intelligently. Perhaps he will give us some clues, which we would never suspect, if we didn't know. We have a foothold, Bjarne, in the fact that we know Leif Hunseid as he really is."

"You mean, because we know and he doesn't know that we know?"

"That's right, Bjarne?"

"You've a real strategy, Prest Gran! We do have a foothold!"

"And now let us be patient! Promise me you will be patient, Bjarne! Promise me!"

"I'll try!"

"Good boy! We must deal cautiously with the enemy, Bjarne. They took us by trickery; perhaps we can meet them on that ground... if we are careful with our information."

"You are a soldier, Prest Gran!"

"And I'm on the winning side! Thank God for that, Bjarne! Our Captain, the Lord Jesus, will never see defeat, nor we with Him!"

They proceeded to the house.

"Shall I tell Borghild?"

"Yes, Bjarne. Keep no secrets from her. She's trustworthy. Sigurd is, too, but... his tongue."

"I understand. We three, only, will know."

They entered the house, where Borghild waited for them. They told her all they had seen and heard.

Twelve

TWO DAYS PASSED as one, and the morning of the second day gave early place to afternoon. As the sun slipped rapidly westward, Borghild envied Joshua.

She spent most of the afternoon in her room, pacing, nibbling nervously at the tips of her fingers, groping for courage, battling fear.

Bruno Schreckenbach would be waiting for her, waiting at the cemetery, waiting in the shadows. She was afraid to meet him. She could not. Yet she felt that she must! She must meet him... in the cemetery... in the shadows... alone. No! No! She could not betray Bjarne! Wonderful Bjarne! Their love had not grown cold, though the recent past had divided one's emotions, and days often passed without more than one brief caress.

Of course, she would not betray Bjarne. But could she not betray Schreckenbach? Could she not be a Delilah and sap from him the strength of Nazism and free Bjerkely? Delilah? She was not that kind of a woman. She could not be. In the mirror she caught a glimpse of herself, of the lips spent only on words spelled in a heart that was clean, of the eyes that had always sought that which was pure and of God, of the body that was virtuous. She could not... Or were there times like this when God would forgive a woman, if she betrayed that she might betray, gave herself that she might free others?

"No, dear God!" she wept, as she fell to her knees beside her bed and clutched the spread her mother had crocheted. "Oh, I couldn't, God, I couldn't! But isn't there some way I can use this opportunity, some way I can make that horrible man help me free Bjerkely... and Norway? Guide me, Lord! Guide me! I feel I must go and meet him, Lord. Why do I feel that I must? I'm so afraid! Please help me, Lord! Please help me! Give Thy angels charge over me, Lord! Protect me! Help me! In Jesus' Name... amen."

It was several moments before she could stand again. A quiet peace had approached her, and she breathed deeply, trying to force that assurance close to her faint heart.

She would meet Bruno Schreckenbach tonight. That decision had finality about it.

Hans Laub had the men at the water front busy with camouflaging—making the concrete docks. look once more like fishing wharfs, covering artillery placements with frame warehouse buildings, launching fishing boats to give the final touch of deception. The men were kept at work until eight o'clock each night, because Hans Laub was eager to complete his mission. Birgit, therefore, did not serve supper until dusk, after Bjarne came home.

It was late afternoon, and to make it pass hurriedly, Borghild wandered into Lars' room—little changed from when he had occupied it.

His Bible lay on the table beside the bed. On that table, too, was his pocketknife, a picture, clipped from a newspaper, of Paavo Nurmi, the Finnish track star who had been his hero, and two glass marbles.

"Dear Lars!" Borghild choked.

It was no use to forbid the tears.

When she had had her cry, she went to his bookcase. Grimm's Fairy Tales, a book of Bible stories illustrated, a volume of traditional stories about the Norse gods, and the juvenile works of Hawthorne caught her attention from among the worn volumes. Lars had always loved books. Musing, she remembered reading Treasure Island to him—how tense he had become when Jim Hawkins hid in the apple barrel; and Jonathan Swift's deft satires with Gulliver, from Brobdingnag to Lilliput; and Swiss Family Robinson; and, of course, Robinson Crusoe; besides the best of them all, so far as Lars was concerned, stories of the Vikings, and of Frithjof. Lars had been interested in philately, too. She took his stamp album from the shelf and leafed through its pages. Here was the famed German inflation issue— Lars had never quite believed that one of those stamps was once actually worth those millions of marks. Here was his collection from India. Now Jamaica—his largest stamp was from there—Luxembourg, Malay Peninsula, Norway. He had saved uncanceled stamps from Norway, especially of the commemoratives; each stamp was carefully mounted in a cellophane-like pouch. Turning a few pages, she came to his Swedish collection. He had always begged their father, mother and her to write often to the many relatives of the Gran family in Sweden, because each reply meant another member for his philatelic Scandinavians. A cousin of theirs in Stockholm, a girl a few years younger than she, had first interested Lars in the hobby, and they had often traded from their collections; and whenever they corresponded, they used nothing but commemoratives, of course. Borghild closed the album and was about to return it to its place. But as she did, she was thinking. Lars. Their relatives in Sweden—it would be nice to contact them—from whom they had not heard since the occupation, as there was no mail service to Bjerkely. Stamps. Commemoratives. How was it that Lars took canceled commemoratives from envelopes Without damaging them? Yes, she remembered now.

She opened the album again, and opened it to the collection of unused commemoratives from Norway. A smile trickled from her mouth. She took the album into her room and hid it where no one would find it... including the Gestapo agents, if they should search the town again.

Then she went downstairs.

And the smile was larger now, and growing.

"Getting supper, Birgit?" she asked in the kitchen.

"Yes."

"Mmmmm! *Faarestek*? Smells like it anyway!"

Birgit nodded. "Food is to be rationed here soon, and so I want us to eat well while we can."

"You haven't taken one of my pet lambs, have you?" Borghild teased.

Opening the oven, and pointing at the roast, Birgit said, "No, but the way that Laub does things, I'd say that he'll take cows, lambs, chickens and all from us, if he needs them."

"Let's hope not." She yawned. "That aroma, Birgit! It does things for my appetite!"

Birgit was pleased. She was one of those rare women who have never had a desire for romance, and whose maternal instincts seem to have been transferred to the zest for cookery. Praise for her dishes was the only approach that could bring a glow to her face akin to beauty, and then one had to strain his imagination.

But she could cook, and Sigurd, Who had spent quite some time in the kitchen during the first few weeks after Prest Gran employed him, triumphantly sighed his admission of defeat as a suitor, "Maybe she doesn't know how to fall in love, but she can cook, and I'm satisfied!"

After a glance at the window, Borghild said, "There comes Bjarne!"

"Supper will be ready in five minutes," Birgit said.

"No hurry," Borghild told her, as she ran out to meet Bjarne... looking, as she did, toward the cemetery, as though a magnet drew her eyes that way.

"Hello, sweetheart," he mumbled, as she came to him.

"Hello, Bjarne." She kissed him, briefly, and then asked, taking his arm to walk at his side, "Hard work today, dear?"

"Yes," he moaned, "another hour and I would have dropped. The last gun was mounted today. The derrick broke down, and rather than wait two days or so for repairs, Laub made a dozen of us younger men slide it into position."

"Without a machine, Bjarne?"

"Yes. It must have weighed at least three tons."

"Oh, how horrible!"

"If the tide ever turns, I pity Hans Laub!"

They walked a few steps in silence. Borghild threw her head back toward the cemetery. It fascinated her, made her eager to meet Bruno Schreckenbach!

"Is the work nearly finished?" she asked.

He nodded. "Trucks are already bringing supplies to be kept in the warehouses."

"Supplies?"

"For the submarines."

"Oh. What?"

"Food. Torpedoes... beastly looking things. Laub has confiscated those fuel tanks of Johan Berge's. One crew started work today digging a pit to submerge them in."

"Fuel for the submarines?"

He nodded. "And I suppose we'll have to roll them in there without the help of a derrick."

"You poor men!"

"You haven't seen Leif Hunseid today?"

She bit her lips, before saying, "No. I dread thinking of him."

"If anyone had tried to make me believe that he, of all men, would do a thing like that . . ."

"It is unbelievable."

"He's got this town so fooled that if we were to try to expose him, he might be able to convince the people that we were lying."

"No use exposing him now, Bjarne. Remember what Father said, when you told me about him last night... we have a foothold now, at least. We've got something to work on anyway."

"I wonder what good it's going to do us."

"Be patient, Bjarne!"

They entered the house.

Borghild whispered, "Leif Hunseid is visiting Father." '

They went to the two men.

Leif Hunseid stood. "Hello, Bjarne. Worn out, aren't you?"

"He surely is," Borghild said, fearing that Bjarne, extremely fatigued, might betray their secret.

"That man Hans Laub," Leif Hunseid said through grating teeth, "is the nearest thing to a beast I've seen!"

"When man betrays his soul to Satan," Prest Gran said, "he sometimes becomes lower than the beasts."

Leif Hunseid twitched.

"Bjarne said," Borghild broke the silence, "that today a derrick broke down and so he and eleven other young men had to finish mounting a three-ton gun with their hands."

"Is that true, Bjarne?" Leif asked.

Bjarne nodded.

The mayor beat his palm with his opposite fist, "Hasn't he any sense of decency? Thank God things have gone smoothly at the fjord, so there haven't been more atrocities!"

"We men know there's nothing to do but subject ourselves," Bjarne said. "If only we had guns!"

"Don't remind me!" Leif Hunseid begged. "I've spent more than half of the nights since the invasion without sleeping a wink, Bjarne... lying there all night thinking of what we might have been able to do if I hadn't called that meeting, when the Nazis kept us prisoners in the church until they had disarmed the town. But how was I to know? I thought Schreckenbach and the rest of his men had gone to Oslo to join the fight there. Who would ever have thought that Bjerkely was a key objective of the Nazis!"

"Nobody," Bjarne shrugged, "unless there might have been Quislingers in Bjerkely."

Borghild hastened, "But there isn't one! Do you suspect anyone, Mr. Hunseid?"

"The people of Bjerkely are faithful Norwegians to the last man! ...Don't you agree with me, Prest Gran?"

"It has seemed so."

"You... don't suspect anyone, do you?"

"Of course not, Mr. Hunseid!" Borghild assured.

"I know I haven't!" Leif Hunseid calmed noticeably. "If only there were some way to ruin Laub's plans here. Prest Gran, how can we sit here, doing nothing in protest, While our beloved Bjerkely is made a Nazi submarine base?"

"We must be patient, Leif," Prest Gran said. "We must be patient, willing to wait for the strategic moment to attack."

"Do you have any suggestions," the mayor asked, "as to how we might go about an attack? I've thought we should make an effort to get news to England, perhaps, so the R. A. F. could bomb the fjord."

"That would suit me!" Bjarne thrilled.

"But how could we do it?" Leif Hunseid asked.

"That's just the question," Borghild said, "how could we do it?"

"Perhaps the opportunity will come," Prest Gran said.

"Perhaps," Leif Hunseid continued, "but it's impossible to get any mail out of Bjerkely. I've tried to talk Laub and Schreckenbach into letting us send letters under a board of censorship, but they insist that every precaution must be kept to prevent the British from learning of Bjerkely. And it's impossible to try to break past the sentries. Laub and Schreckenbach have the name of every man, woman and child in Bjerkely on file. If anyone were missing, we'd have a reign of terror here worse than the Inquisition."

"We can pray," the minister assured, "and we can be sure that God will provide an answer for every need."

"Uh... yes," from Hunseid. "Have you heard, Bjarne, that Laub is taking Johan's fuel tanks to be used on the U-boat base?"

"The men began digging pits for them today," Bjarne answered.

"They've taken control of everything. The grocery shelves won't be restocked until after next week when all *stabbur* supplies are checked—and you know how empty they are this time of the year —and all cattle, pigs and sheep registered. I'm looking for a hard winter, unless something is done. Why don't the British try a counter invasion?"

"Give them time," Bjarne said.

"I suppose," Leif Hunseid admitted, "we should be patient." Then he continued, "You should see my hotel. You men haven't been there since the invasion, have you?"

"We," Prest Gran said, "haven't visited you, Leif. We—"

"Come sometime... that is, if the Gestapo sentries will let you in. There are swastikas on the walls of every room, while I sit there, helpless."

"Supper!" Birgit called.

"Will you eat with us, Leif?" the minister asked.

"Uh... no. Thank you, but... I must get back to the hotel. I'll go."

"We would—"

"No. Honestly, I must go."

He left, and the family went to the table.

When the meal was over, Bjarne sighed, "If you will excuse me, I'll go to bed."

"Of course, Bjarne," Borghild smiled.

"You need rest," Prest Gran added.

"I'm going to weed potatoes," Sigurd said.

And so they separated.

Borghild went outside immediately. It was dusk, now, and shadows were everywhere. She hurried to the cemetery.

Bruno Schreckenbach lurked in the darkest shadows. When she saw him, her first impulse was to turn back. But, bold as the bravest Norwegian warrior, she went toward him, determined to perform her mission.

"Miss Gran! I knew you would come!"

He held out his arms, inviting her to them.

"No!" she protested.

"Please!" he begged, coming toward her.

But as he touched her, she pushed him gently, but firmly, away. "I have come to talk," she said. "You promised you would be a gentleman. You can keep promises, can't you?"

"Of course I can!"

He stepped back.

"Thank you."

"You are so beautiful," he whispered. "In all Germany, I have never seen a woman so beautiful! I love you! I love you, Miss Gran!"

His eyes stood out against the shadows, eager and demanding. He was trembling, and Borghild thought she saw the fist of his heart bulging against his brown shirt.

"Mr. Schreckenbach," she began, "how could you ever expect a Norwegian girl, unless she were a Quislinger, to love you?"

"I...I...uh—"

"Women love men who are dominant, but never despotic."

"But, Miss Gran, I haven't—"

Each time he spoke, she used the time for prayer.

"You are a deluded man, Mr. Schreckenbach! Nazism has so stained your personality that... that I doubt if you will ever be normal again. You—"

"What do you mean?"

"You have brought Nazi tactics to your love-making! Nazism has stained you to your depths—to your soul!"

"I—"

"You want to steal the love of one betrothed to another, just as your armies have——"

"Miss Gran, you don't understand! You—"

"I am a Christian, Bruno Schreckenbach! But even if I weren't —unless I, too, had fallen the pray of Nazism —I would have heart enough not to attempt stealing another's love! I—"

"Miss Gran, listen to me!"

"You—"

"Listen to me, Miss Gran!"

He was Bruno Schreckenbach, the Nazi, now... Bruno Schreckenbach of the Gestapo. He demanded. and she obeyed.

"I will listen," she said.

"You think that we Nazis are driven by greed. You are wrong. We want only that there should be justice, or at least an example of justice, in the world. But what if we were driven by greed? What if it were true that I am the greedy monster you think me to be?" He was the Bruno Schreckenbach, now, who loved Borghild Gran. "Isn't love a greater force than greed?"

"It—"

"Have you never loved someone enough to see that it is possible to be so entranced by love, so absolutely enslaved by the quest for another's heart, that you would give all you hold dear to win that one?" He burned his eyes against hers with the fury of a flamethrower. "Haven't you known love like that, Miss Gran?"

"I—"

"I have!" He whispered once more. "I have found that kind of love here in Norway! I love you, Miss Gran! I love so much that I want you... want you at any price! Any price, Miss Gran! Only to have you!"

The night shadows could not hide his sincerity. For a moment, he, the ugly Gestapo agent, resembled her father, she thought, when he made his most earnest pleas to the souls of men. No one had doubted the sincerity of Prest Gran.

Borghild could not doubt Bruno Schreckenbach's sincerity.

"Believe me, Miss Gran," he whispered, taking her hand into the vice of his own, "I love you enough to— to," he labored for breath, "betray my country!"

"Mr. Schreckenbach!" she gasped.

"I am your slave, Miss Gran," he whispered, "I am your slave. Betray me, if you will. Use me to rid Bjerkely of Hans Laub, if you will. Use me to—"

"You are jealous of Hans Laub?"

"Miss Gran!"

"If you were to give me a gun, and," she sneered, "perhaps I could convince Bjarne to kill Laub, you wouldn't be held responsible. And Bjarne would be executed. That would please you!"

"Miss Gran! How dare you—"

"Is it true?"

"I swear it isn't! Can't you see that I love you!" He pleaded earnestly, his words vitalized by the glow of a face which Borghild knew was sincere. "I love you, Miss Gran! I love you!"

She could not meet his eyes, nor could she withdraw her hand.

"I must go," she said, trying to free herself.

"I will let you go," he whispered. "You are my master, I am your slave."

She trembled.

"Would it make you happy," he asked, "if I would help you to get rid of Hans Laub? If I would be a traitor to—"

"Aren't you convinced that Nazism is the ideal?"

"Yes, but it is below love."

"Could you love a woman, if she refused you her love until you were willing to betray something you believed in, something you thought would benefit the world? Could you love a woman like that?"

"You... you have the wisdom of your father, ...the way to say things that perplex me. I..."

"You need my Christ, Mr. Schreckenbach. You need to confess your sins, accept Christ as your Saviour, and be born again. Do you understand terms like that?"

He had nothing to say.

"That conflicts with Nazi doctrine, doesn't it?"

He remained silent.

"You are very arrogant, on the surface, but you are meek within. All Nazis are that way, aren't they? When the tide of battle turns, and the inevitable defeat looms before them, all Nazis will be soft, won't they?"

"I have an appointment," he excused. "Will you meet me tomorrow night? Will you meet me here... tomorrow night?"

She turned from him.

"I will be here," he called. "Will you meet me?"

She increased the distance between them. Presently, she was running.

Bruno Schreckenbach returned, through the shadows, to the hotel. He went to the suite occupied by Hans Laub. Leif Hunseid and Laub were sitting by the mock fireplace, where an electrical resemblance of embers glowed.

"Back, are you?" Hans Laub asked.

"Well," Hunseid chuckled, "has she promised to be Frau Schreckenbach?"

The two waited silently for him to speak.

He did not speak.

"What progress did you make?" Laub demanded.

With the sincerity in his eyes that Borghild had seen, he said, "She is a beautiful girl! She is—"

"Schreckenbach! You fool! Are you going to let silly sentiment —"

"We went over that, Hans," Schreckenbach interrupted. "I trust you."

"Tell me, did you offer to help get rid of me? Did you tell her that?"

"Yes... I did."

"What did she say?"

"She... she began talking about ideals, about being true to what one believes... about—"

"Oh, prattle! That's a woman for you!"

"I tell you—"

"Sure, I know, Bruno, you love her. That's fine. That's splendid. Did she reveal any plans? Have the people any plans for getting rid of me? Have they, Bruno?"

"I couldn't get her to say. I... I was very easy with her tonight."

"Listen, Schreckenbach," Hans Laub whined, "this is clear. I'm telling you for the last time. You are going to take this Gran girl with you back to Germany when the war is over! Even if she is the one who originates the plot, she will be left unharmed! Is that clear? Or will I have to tell you again in a couple of hours? We'll get rid of this Kolstad fellow for you, and the old man Gran, if necessary, but if we execute everybody in Bjerkely, we won't harm the girl!"

"I believe you, Hans!" Schreckenbach was impatient. "I'm doing my best! I offered to help her! She'll come my way!"

"You are seeing her again?"

"I told her to meet me in the cemetery tomorrow night."

"Did she say she would come?"

"She didn't say she would come tonight, but she did."

Laub demanded, "Did she promise to meet you?"

"She didn't promise."

"Fool! Can't—"

"I couldn't"make her promise against her will!"

"You—"

"Leave it to me, Hans! I'll work out everything!"

"Sure you will, Bruno! Sure you will!" Laub's eyes narrowed to slits. "You see, the Führer himself is interested in Bjerkely! I am responsible to the Führer! That responsibility was given to me four years ago, when Hunseid reported the possibility of a submarine base here in the event of a war with England! That's why I am so determined to crush any effort to thwart our plans... now that we have proceeded so splendidly!"

"I am going to my room."

"Yes, go ahead, Bruno. You will need to make plans... for tomorrow night."

Schreckenbach went to the door.

"Heil Hitler, Bruno!" Hans Laub shouted.

"Heil Hitler!" Schreckenbach mumbled, and left the room.

He paced about his room until midnight, thinking constantly of her. He wondered if he could trust Hunseid and Laub. He wondered if they would leave Borghild for him, after they had taken whatever toll of life might be necessary to make Bjerkely the great submarine base they intended it to be. Certainly, they would keep their promises! Why should he not trust them? They trusted him. Surging thrills swept over him. Borghild Gran! Beautiful Miss Gran! She was to be his spoil! That was worth every effort!

Contented at last, he retired... to find her in his dreams—not obstinate there, but his, by her own choice.

Thirteen

BORGHILD ANTICIPATED the evening shadows. At intervals she would go to her window to see how much farther the shadow of the church spire had penetrated into the cemetery.

She was writing a letter... to her cousin... the cousin in Stockholm... the cousin whose hobby was stamp collecting.

She wrote:

Dear Kisa,

I have wanted to write to you sooner, but the events of the recent past have upset things here, and mail service has been quite poor. In fact, I am quite certain you couldn't get a letter to me, so don't write, at least until you hear from me again.

We are well, Father and I. But that is the extent of the good news from our family. It will shock you, and the others, to learn that Lars very suddenly passed away a few weeks ago. Father took it so magnificently. Perhaps it is best that way.

We are happy. The gardens are good this year. We haven't been to the woods this summer, too busy. Perhaps it won't be long until you can visit Bjerkely again, and we can take a long hike through the woods.

Greet all from us. God bless you richly.

Your cousin,

Borghild

She folded the letter and slipped it into a plain envelope.

Then she addressed the envelope. She addressed it carefully, using the permanent black ink her father used for keeping the church records, filling out marriage certificates, and making notes in his Bible. Her father was calling in his parish this afternoon, and so she had taken the ink to her room. She would return it before he came home.

Lars' stamp album was opened to Norway. The collection was almost complete; it was complete of the most recent commemoratives. Borghild hesitated a moment before she removed the ten-ore Queen Maud memorial from its hinge, moistened it, and very carefully placed it on the letter to Stockholm.

She dropped to her knees, and, clutching the letter to her heart, begged her God to see it safely to its destination.

When she arose, she had confidence. After hiding the letter beneath her pillow, and once more returning Lars' stamp album to the bookshelf in his room, she descended the stairs, and returned the ink to her father's study.

Bjarne was home. He sat, partly slumped, in a chair by the fireplace. Furrows of fatigue had plowed the youthful glow from his face. He needed to shave. His eyes were loathe to move.

"Poor dear Bjarne!" Borghild sympathized, going to him. She ran her fingers through his hair, supported his chin with her other hand, stooped and placed a warm kiss on each of his cheeks.

He sighed, looked up at her, smiled.

"Too tired to talk almost, aren't you?"

He nodded.

"Was the work as hard today?"

"Harder. We installed those big fuel tanks. Laub had them pulled over by a tractor, but we had to erect a hand derrick for lowering the tanks into the pits that were dug."

"How terrible."

"Gynt Berg, the young fellow (can't be over nineteen), got his leg caught when we were doing it. We had to pull one of the tanks up by hand, or his leg would have been crushed."

"Did he break his leg?"

"His father said it was fractured. Laub accused Doctor of calling it a fracture, so his boy wouldn't be forced to work at the project any longer. Leif Hunseid was down there, and he took the doctor's part."

"Thank God it wasn't worse."

"Yes," Bjarne sighed. "Pay day again today. That is, we get the receipts that tell us how much we've done for the Nazis!"

"Not good Norwegian money by any chance?"

"No chance!" Bjarne sneered, pulling an occupational certificate from his envelope. "But then Leif Hunseid told some of us men that he is permitted, when the rationing comes in, to buy supplies for his store with the certificates. It all works out beautifully... for the Nazis, doesn't it? Hunseid gets to buy supplies with the occupational currency. The people, who don't know what a Judas he is, will think that gives value to the trash. They'll be willing to work all the harder. And so the Nazis profit!"

"Too bad there aren't farms here along the fjord, so we—"

"If there were, the Nazis would have chosen some other fishing port for their base. Bjerkely's ideal for the sentries. A man couldn't break through their guard no matter how hard he tried. And," once more he sighed, "as long as we can't break their guard, it's no use hoping that we can get a message to the R. A. F. to bomb the base."

Behind the frown on her face, Borghild was smiling.

When supper was over, Bjarne said, "If I weren't so dead tired, sweetheart, we'd go for a walk, but..."

"I understand, dear. It won't be much longer that you'll have to work so hard. Then, perhaps."

"Then," he growled, "we'll be kept busy servicing submarines, I suppose!"

"Don't be so despondent, dear. You know how the reports from Narvik, and on into the coal country, tell of resistance. Bridges are weakened, so that they collapse under Nazi loads. Railroad ties are sprung out of shape. Communication wires are cut. There will be ways for us to resist... I'm sure there will be!"

"If you could spend the hours I spend, being watched constantly by the Gestapo guards, your Optimism wouldn't thrive so well, dear."

She smiled.

"I'll be going to bed," he yawned. "See you in the morning, sweetheart."

"Good night, Bjarne."

She kissed him, watched him ascend the stairs to his room. Then she tiptoed upstairs, into her room, where she took the letter from underneath her pillow, descended the stairs, and went outside.

Sigurd was finishing a few of the chores not done before supper.

"Going for a walk?" he asked.

"Yes. I... I'm going to wander through the cemetery."

"Pretty this time of year. How are the flowers we planted on Lars' grave?"

"They're growing every day, Sigurd."

He scowled, "That boy shouldn't be in his grave!"

"Don't feel that way about it. God knows what is—"

"I'm not thinking of it that way," he explained. "What I mean is, if the Nazis would have left us alone, so we could go about our ways the way we always had, there wouldn't have been—"

"No use dreaming of what might have been."

"Guess not," he admitted.

"I've heard that things are quite normal in some parts of Norway. Oslo and Bergen, for instance."

Sigurd chuckled, "I've heard them tell that Quisling has opened the theaters in Oslo. And the other night a comedian walked to the front of the platform and gave the Nazi salute. Right away about a hundred Quislingers stood, and returned the salute with a husky "Heil Hitler!" He giggled, "The comedian yelled at them, 'You interrupted me! I was about to say, that's how high my dog jumped yesterday!' That was his last performance... but it was his best."

"I think I'll be going," she said, as the *dreng* picked up a couple of buckets and went toward the barn.

"Don't be gone too long. Too many Nazis around here!"

"Don't worry!"

The shadow of the church spire stretched completely across the cemetery, like a long arm clutching a cross. She was alone... alone in the shadows cast by the Gran family stone.

Looking, with eyes moist from the overflow of her cup of praise, at the shadow of the church cross, she softly sang:

> In the Cross of Christ I glory,
> Tow'ring o'er the wrecks of time;
> All the light of sacred story
> Gathers round its head sublime.
>
> When the woes of life o'ertake me,
> Hopes deceive, and fears annoy,
> Never shall the Cross forsake me:
> Lo! it glows with peace and joy.
>
> When the sun of bliss is beaming
> Light and love upon my way,
> From the Cross, the radiance streaming
> Adds more luster to the day.
>
> Bane and blessing, pain and pleasure,
> By the Cross are sanctified;
> Peace is there that knows no measure,
> Joys that thro' all time abide.

As she sang, she remembered her Father's sermon last Sabbath. He had said, "It is not Scriptural for the Christian to go to the Cross for forgiveness of sin. It is not Scriptural for us to seek there the balm for our wounded souls. It is an emblem of what He did for us, but it is not the source of what He now does for us." She seemed to hear him now, see the way his face had caught the glow of his message. "The Christian is admonished by the Word of God, that, seeing then that we have a great high priest, that is passed into the heavens, Jesus the Son of God, let us hold fast our profession. For we have not an high priest which cannot be touched with the feeling of our infirmities; but was in all points tempted like as we are, yet without sin. Let us therefore come boldly unto the throne of grace, that we may obtain mercy, and find grace to help in time of need. Here we are told of the Christian and temptation... the trials and testings which beset us so sorely today... but we are not told to bring them to the Cross, but rather DIRECTLY TO THE THRONE OF GRACE, which is in heaven! The poor, penitent sinner pleads for mercy at the Cross, but the regenerated saint may come boldly to the throne of grace!"

She fell to her knees—one knee on the grave of her mother, the other on Lars'—and sent her petitions to the throne of grace.

Lifting her head heavenward, after her prayer, she began to sing:

> My faith looks up to Thee,
> Thou Lamb of Calvary,
> Saviour divine!
> Now hear me while I pray,
> Take all my guilt away,
> O let me from this day
> Be wholly Thine!
> May Thy rich grace impart—"

"You sing beautifully, Miss Gran!"

"Oh!" Quickly, she stood. "Mr. Schreckenbach! I—"

"I didn't intend to frighten you," he apologized.

The heat of his eyes had been intensified since, last she saw him. There was more determination in the lines that sprang from his lips, and less of his former hesitance. His breath was that of a seasoned runner.

For a moment, she was afraid—until she spent another moment at the throne of grace.

"You came," he thrilled. "I knew you would! You came to me, Miss Gran!"

"Yes, I—"

"You are not so obstinate? You tell me you dislike me," he smiled, "yet you come to me!"

He took her arms and pulled her toward him.

"No!" she protested.

It was no use, for he locked her in the prison of his arms. But she turned her lips from him, and his kisses went to her hair.

"Please!" she begged. "Please, or I'll scream for help!"

He released her. "You are an interesting woman. You come to me, and I make love to you, and you try to get away." There was no tone of discouragement in his words. "Why do you come to me, if you don't seek my love... as much as I seek yours?"

"I...I..."

Again he drew her to him. "Come! I must hurry back! Let us not waste the valuable time!"

"Don't!" she protested, and tried to push herself free. But it was no use.

"Why do you deny me your lips?" he whispered.

She could feel the anvil-blows of his heart, the expansion of his chest as storms of breath bulged his lungs. His arms trembled. His thick fingers stroked her shoulders.

"Please! Please, Mr. Schreckenbach! Please!"

"You do not want to go! Turn your lips to me, Miss Gran! Beautiful Miss Gran!"

"Let me go, please! You said," she fought him, "you were a gentleman!"

That turned the key to the door of his embrace.

"You... you do not want me to love you?" he asked, his face white, his dark eyes contrasting with the whiteness.

"I...I..."

"Then—"

"I must hurry back. My people know I came to the cemetery. They—"

"Did you tell them you came to meet me?" he demanded.

"No! Of course I didn't! Bjarne," (the mention of his name thrilled through her palsied form and gave her courage!) "B-Bjarne would object, if I told him."

"You only said you were going for a walk?"

"Yes."

He seemed relieved.

"But I must go soon. Really I must."

"I shouldn't complain," he smiled, "when you are so kind to come to me. I am very eager... because I love you so much. But I will be patient. I will wait for your heart to mold to mine. I will be patient, Miss Gran. I will be patient."

Bluntly, she said, "I Wish you would do me a favor."

"A favor? Anything! You... you want me to help you destroy Hans Laub? You want me to help—"

"No! I am. content to leave judgments to God!"

"Then... what do you want?"

From the pocket of her apron-like skirt, she took the envelope... the envelope addressed in permanent ink... the envelope stamped with a Norwegian commemorative.

"A letter?" he asked.

"Yes. Can you send it for me?"

"But—"

"It's to our relatives in Stockholm, written to my cousin. They will be wondering about us, and—"

"Does your father know you are trying to send this through me?" he snapped. "Does he know you are seeing me?"

"No, I—"

"Are you lying to me?"

"Before God, Mr. Schreckenbach, I tell the truth."

"I believe you," he said. "You aren't trying to send information to—"

"The enverope is unsealed," she said. "You may read it."

She handed it to him."

"But perhaps you use code."

"Code?" she laughed. "When would simple people like us here in Bjerkely learn—?"

"You will forgive me, please. As a member of the Gestapo, and of the Nazi Party, I must be careful."

"Will you mail it for me?"

"Tonight. The dispatches leave tonight. I am positive that I can send this with them."

"Will Hans Laub—?"

"He knows that I see you," Schreckenback blurted. "H...he..."

"Oh!"

"He doesn't object. He trusts me. So," he smiled, "if I can help you... and be rewarded by your love... I—"

"You promise to send the letter? It would mean so much to my relatives in Stockholm!"

"I give you my word, Miss Gran, that the letter will reach them safely! There is a Board of Censorship in Oslo, but if you have written nothing forbidden, there will be no difficulty. I assure you."

"Thank you! Now I must go."

"So soon?"

She turned, began walking away.

"You will come back tomorrow night?" he begged. "I have proved that I am a gentleman."

She continued walking.

"You will come back, Miss Gran? You will come back?"

She did not answer.

"I know you will! I will be waiting! I will have more time tomorrow night! I will be waiting, Miss Gran! I will be waiting!"

She ran ,to the church. There, secluded against the church steps, she fell to her knees. "Dear God, how can I thank Thee! Guide the letter, Lord! Guide it! Please, dear God! Please!"

She ran home.

Leif Hunseid was in Hans Laub's suite at the hotel, where they were finishing plans for the food rationing. "You're sure there are enough ration cards, Leif?"

"And a few to spare."

"Good!"

"You only intend to issue food cards?"

"Of course," Laub laughed. "By winter there not only will be no clothing for the Norwegians, but their jackets, sweaters, topcoats and all bedding will be confiscated. Demands are heavy in Germany."

"Does that include the hotel bedding?" Leif chuckled.

"We'll empty all of the spare rooms, store the bedding in the basement, and then carry out empty boxes, so everybody will be fooled. But there'll be bedding to spare for all the rooms that are occupied. Well, do we have the ration program worked out?"

"As far as I know, Hans."

"Plenty clever, eh, Leif? The people think you're taking a beating right along with them! They think you lose on the occupational certificates, the same as they do!"

There was knocking at the door.

"Bruno?"

"Yes."

"Come in."

Bruno Schreckenbach entered.

"You saw her tonight?"

"Yes, Hans."

"Good! The girl must be infatuated with you! They say girls love men in uniforms!"

"Don't you have a couple of extra uniforms?" Leif Hunseid joked.

"What headway did you make, Bruno?"

Bruno Schreckenbach grinned.

"You kissed her?" Laub sang.

"Yes."

"Splendid! What else? Did she reveal any plots?"

"No. I tell you, Hans, I don't believe there are any plots. That girl has complete trust in me, and... and—"

"And what?"

"She said the people are Willing to leave judgment to God."

Hans Laub shook with the laughter that crowded through his mouth and oozed from his nose. "So they're planning to sic God on me, are they? Looks like I'll need to arm my bodyguards with antiaircraft guns!"

Schreckenbach tried, but he could not join their laughter. He covered his mouth with his hand, to hide his sobriety.

"Anything else?" Hans Laub asked, after he had calmed. "She didn't say what day God would be after me, did she?"

"She gave me this letter."

"Letter? Let me see it." Taking it from Schreckenbach, he exclaimed, "Man, this is addressed to Stockholm! What is this, a plot?"

"Read it. She wants her relatives to know that she and her father are well and... happy. It strikes me," Schreckenbach said, "as a fine opportunity to keep the truth of this town hidden."

"What do you mean?"

"The letter."

"Hmmm. But it probably wouldn't reach outside of the house where it is sent." He opened it, and read it aloud. "Not a chance of any information getting through a letter like that, is there?"

"Not a chance."

"You know, Bruno, this gives me a splendid idea. We've got to establish mail delivery here again, now that things are organized as they are. I never once thought of how tragic it might be if relatives of the Bjerkely people, relatives in Sweden for instance, began to suspect trouble here, now that Sweden receives mail from other parts of Norway. It all has to be censored, so what danger is there? And then it might help the morale of the people here, if they got mail. What do you think, Leif?"

"We could play it up this way, Hans. We'll get the word around that I have begged you to establish postal connections again so—"

"Say, that's a great idea, Leif! What do you think, Bruno? Clever, isn't it?"

"Yes. Clever."

Hans Laub said, "There are dozens of mail sacks in Oslo, all for Bjerkely. That ought to please the people, if we'd have it brought here and distributed. It's all been censored."

"Great thinking there, Laub!" Hunseid praised.

"I'll make arrangements tonight."

"Shall," Bruno Schreckenbach hesitated, "I... send this letter with tonight's dispatches, or wait until mail service is restored?"

"Send it tonight! No harm in that, is there, Leif?"

"Not that I can see."

Laub said, "I left the dispatches on your desk, Bruno." He looked at his watch. "The truck will be leaving for Oslo in another hour. Can you have your reports ready by then?"

"Yes. I haven't much to report."

"You aren't sorry, Bruno, that the Gestapo hasn't had to enforce penalties on the people?"

"No, I—"

"The less of that that's necessary," Hunseid laughed, "the more sure he is of winning the Gran girl. That right, Bruno?"

Bruno Schreckenbach grinned.

"We have ration plans worked out, Bruno," Hans Laub informed. "I'm glad we didn't need to cut supplies before the U-boat base was completed. We might have had trouble getting the men to work."

"When does the rationing begin?"

"Two more days... Monday."

Schreckenbach excused, "I must go. You'll excuse me, please."

"Surely."

Hans Laub said, "Good work, Bruno! I'm proud of you! Some day I shall suggest that the Führer decorate you with the highest honors of the Third Reich!"

"Thank you, Hans."

He left the suite and went to his office; but before preparing his dispatches to Gestapo headquarters in Oslo and Berlin, he read once more Borghild's letter. He could see her beauty personified in the handwriting. It was as though the ink had been perfume, for thoughts of her, as he read, suggested a quiet home in one of

Berlin's suburbs, or, perhaps, at Bremen, on the sea, where flowers she would plant would make him forget the bloody price he might have to pay for her love.

He clutched the letter to his heart, sealed it, gazed at her handwriting on the outside, clutched it to his heart again.

Then he began his work.

Fourteen

BORGHILD WENT FROM the supper table to her room. There, not daring to turn on her light, she sat until the sun had burned its way beneath the western horizon, and the last embers of day charred to the gray ashes of dusk.

From her window she could see the cemetery, its gate and the sides that sloped to the valley, the secluded valley, where Lars and her mother were buried. She saw Bruno Schreckenbach slowly descend into that valley, and then, after he had waited half an hour, she saw him come to the cemetery gate beside the churchyard, and look toward the *Prestegaarden*. She saw him coming... coming toward her.

Her heart tossed like a fishing boat in a frenzied fjord. Her breath came in rationed gasps.

Nearer and nearer he came, into the yard, to the house. In a moment, she heard the door chimes.

Except for the strength of youth, she would have fallen dead.

She fell to her knees, but she was too frightened to pray. She could only trust. She tried to get enough strength to call Bjarne, but did not have strength enough to move.

The door chimes sounded again.

Her father called, "Have you returned, Borghild?"

The door chimes sounded a third time.

She heard her father's slow, deliberate steps to the door.

"Mr. Schreckenbach," she heard him say. "What brings you?"

"I... I came for a chat."

"Come in?"

143

"Thank you."

A supply of adrenalin reached her blood. Under its spell, she crawled to the head of the stairs where, shielded by the dark, she could see beneath, without being seen.

Bruno Schreckenbach's eyes were searching every corner. Once they turned up toward her, and her eyes met his! But she knew he could not see her, yet she feared.

Perhaps she should have gone to him. But she could not. It would have killed her to feel his arms about her. Her purpose had been fulfilled. She was sure he had mailed the letter. Now she must never see him alone again.

But What if he were angry? What if, in his fury, he should kill Bjarne? That was a simple procedure for a Gestapo officer.

"Come in," Prest Gran invited below. "Come into the living room."

"You... are alone?" His words drove daggers into her heart.

"No. But I think nearly everyone has retired but me."

Now his eyes were searching the stairway! She buried herself in the darkness that covered the floor.

"You wished to see someone but me, Mr. Schreckenbach?"

"No. I was walking by. I walk each evening. I thought I would come in. But perhaps I had better go."

"Why? Can—"

"You are busy?"

"I was preparing my sermon, but—"

"I will go."

Bluntly, Schreckenbach left the house.

Borghild saw her father stand, puzzled, for a moment, before he returned to his study.

Returning to her window, she was sure she saw him lurking in the shadows about the house. Once she thought she heard him calling. Or was it only the wind? Once she thought she saw a ladder appearing at her window. She scoffed at her imagination. How would he know which was her window? She thought she could see his piercing eyes, divorced from their sockets, roving about the windowpane. With trembling hands, she made sure the window was lOcked. A bug, blinded by the night, struck the glass. To her tense nerves, it was a knocking fist!

Inch by inch, she crept to the opposite side of the room, until she was stopped by the wall. Never had she known such fear. There had been boldness when she had gone to see him. But' it had all left her now. The darkness horrified her, and it seemed longer until morning than it is to dawn when winter has newly begun its reign of darkness above the Arctic Circle.

She did not know how long she sat, cramped against the wall.

It was until her father called, "Borghild, have you retired?"

"I'm in my room," she managed to answer.

"I thought perhaps you were outside, and I was worried. Are you very busy?"

"N—No."

"Could you come down?"

"In a moment."

"I'll be in my study."

She stood, and tried to get her strength through deep breaths. She descended the stairs carefully, lest she fall.

The corridor was dark. She feared darkness. She ran past the door, expecting it to open and give entrance to Bruno Schreckenbach's hands, those hands which, had he had his way, would have drawn her into his embrace tonight.

"What did you want, Father?" she asked, as she opened the study door.

"My dear, what's wrong? You look frightened?"

"Frightened?"

"Your eyes are about to—"

"Oh. I was sitting in the dark. My eyes aren't accustomed to your light yet."

"Sitting in the dark?"

"Thinking."

"I didn't want to interrupt you."

"That's quite all right, Father. I...I'm glad you did."

"You were," he smiled, "thinking about the gloomy side of things?"

"Y-Yes."

He shook his head. "We shouldn't do that, if we can possibly help it. I'm trying to prepare my message for Sunday as an appeal to see things from the bright side. I thought, perhaps, you'd give me your opinion of some of the thoughts I intend to use."

She had inherited this pleasant task from her mother, though, of late, since the invasion, her father had not asked her to go over his sermons with him.

"I'm so glad you asked me, Father."

He was very pleased.

"Your sermons have been of much help to the people."

"I try to keep them close to the Word of God," he smiled. "Perhaps that is why." He opened his Bible. "My subject is 'The God Who Is Equal to Every Trial.'"

"Sounds good, Father."

"My text," his eyes flashed the voltage of his heart, "is the twenty-third Psalm."

Already, she had begun to be more calm.

"The Lord is my shepherd," he began. "He is the One who is equal to every trial! With the help of the Holy Spirit, I hope to bring into my message the teaching of this Psalm as to the way He meets, triumphantly, each trial that may come to the saint. But first, it thrills me to read that he maketh me to lie down in green pastures: he leadeth me beside the still waters. Isn't it wonderful to know that the Lord assures us, even before He enumerates His promises, that we can be at peace, whatever the tempest?"

Borghild's parched soul drank every word!

"He restoreth my soul. That challenges any who seek to destroy us! Trials may make us weary, but the Lord has provided for our spiritual metabolism! Isn't that a precious thought, my dear?"

Her eyes were the only answer he needed.

"He leadeth me in the paths of righteousness for his name's sake. He didn't say where the paths of righteousness might lead us, did He? He only promises that He will lead us in the paths of righteousness! Those paths may lead through the parched deserts of want. They may wind over the steep mountains . of temptation, where one misstep would mean ruin. They may pierce the jungles of oppression, where Satan lurks, eager to destroy us. But, Borghild, dear, He leadeth!"

Tears were wending their way down her pretty cheeks.

"Yea, though I walk through the valley of the shadow of death, I will fear no evil: for thou art with me; thy rod and thy staff they comfort me. Only the valley of the shadow, dear. We can never know real death, for death, though dark as we approach it, through its shadows, is but the portal to the brilliant bliss He has prepared for those who love Him! He may be numbered among the dead in Bjerkely, dear, as those who have given their lives since the occupation." He whispered, "As Lars, Borghild." Tears came, but his smile changed them into a rainbow! "If that comes, I will fear no evil. Glorious thought! For He is with us, guiding us with his rod and his staff. Perhaps you knew that in the Orient, the shepherd went ahead of his flock. And sometimes, when passing the mountains, the sheep would only hear him around a bend, tapping with his staff. That was all the direction they needed! We may not see how near death may be. But He is guiding us!"

The tears were rivers, now, on Borghild's cheeks.

"Thou preparest a table before me in the presence of mine enemies: thou anointest my head with oil; my cup runneth over. Unless the Nazis are driven out, we face a hard winter. They will take many spoils. But even in the presence of our enemies, though they seek to deny us food, He will supply our needs! Surely goodness and mercy shall follow me all the days of my life: and I will dwell in the house of the Lord for ever. Don't you think that Psalm has the message we need, during these difficult days? Food rationing begins Monday, I've been told. The submarine base is ready for activity. But God is still on His throne!"

Borghild dropped to her knees before her father. She leaned forward, resting her head in his lap.

"Father, that's what I've needed! My faith has been so weak! But I'm strengthened! I'm strengthened! The Lord is my shepherd," she looked up at him, "I shall not want."

"Dear girl."

"Thank you so much, Father! Thank you so much!"

Quickly, she stood and, after kissing her father, hurried to her room. She had no fear, now, as she peered out into the darkness. What did it matter if the paths of righteousness led through darkness, so long as the Good Shepherd was leading the way?

She retired, and was soon sleeping as peacefully as she ever had during those tranquil days before the invasion.

Fifteen

BRUNO SCHRECKENBACH was in church on Sunday. Borghild, sitting with Bjarne, felt his eyes stinging her neck. But, had she turned to see, she would have found that, after the Prest began his sermon, Schreckenbach gave much of his attention to the pulpit, and the deeply Spiritual sermon that came upon the congregation as a sharp knife to sinners, a healing balm to saints.

After the services, she and Bjarne walked home together. Turning, once, when she heard heavy footsteps, she saw him... Bruno Schreckenbach... following them. Their eyes met, briefly, for he turned toward the hotel, and they finished the few paces to the parsonage.

Days quickly expanded into weeks. Food rationing came. There was no butter, except what the few Who had cows could churn; very little sugar; chicory was introduced as a substitute for coffee (some had the *Pacha* label on them, the brand label on which the Germans had printed instructions to parachutists in Belgium!), but there were no instructions on these; fats, a rich German source of glycerin for explosives, vanished from the Bjerkely kitchens; the flour had a sawdust taste; all bread was hard, and dry, and wanting flavor; vegetables were a luxury and fruit a memory.

But that was not all. Each family *stabbur—those* small storehouses built on legs above the ground, so that rats and mice cannot transgress, where food is stocked for winter—was searched, and the contents confiscated or itemized. Fish was the only abundant food and the produce from the gardens, though the Germans had their eyes on this.

The submarine base was completed, and, walking along the fjord, one would see a periscope going to sea —the ships came out of the water only at night, or when moved into one of the water-sheds for repair— restocked and refueled, or, as often, moving toward the shore, waiting its turn.

Facts were quite generally known, now, about the armistice at Compiégne, when France fell. Children dropped their toys, the old folk ceased their doting dreams of better years, when tales were spread of the taking to Germany of the 1918 armistice railroad car, after Goering and Hitler, together with officials of the vanquished French, had listened to the new armistice terms, read this time by one named Keitel, a German.

It was now known, also, that a British Expeditionary Force had landed on May 25, captured Narvik May 28, but had been driven entirely out of Norway by June 7. This was but a sample of what the British were going to do, the people of Bjerkely were sure, and each day they waited for news of a mass British invasion which would purge Norway of the Nazis.

But then, with the coming of July, hope dwindled away; for those who had dared listen to news given by the B. B. C., from England, confirmed the Nazi announcements from Berlin that the Battle of Britain was on. Waves of Nazi planes were over England, on reconnaissance flights at first but gradually beginning the most brutal assault of all time.

By the first days of August, the great fight was on. Hundreds of Nazi planes filled the British skies. Naval airfields and dockyards were bombed repeatedly. Residential districts, hospitals—

But why be reminded of the story that is so well known?

It was a midsummer day, late afternoon. At those infrequent moments when a man in uniform was not seen patrolling the streets, Bjerkely was the town of other summers. Her birch branches waved idly in the wind, like mythical nymphs entertaining in the courts of Woden and Thor. Flowers lifted their brilliant heads from the green earth. The woodlands which lined the town on three sides were garbed in the verdant cloak of summer.

But then, when one was beginning to fall under the spell, a Gestapo officer would march past the house, with a gun over his shoulder or a revolver at his side, and all of the beauty became drab.

Borghild and her father were on the veranda.

"If a British plane should fly over," the daughter said, "the pilot would never know but what the men working at the fjord," she pointed to them, "were fishermen."

"It is excellently camouflaged."

"And to think of the tons and tons of concrete, the docks, the supplies. Oh, if only there were a way!"

"If only there were a way!" he echoed.

"Do... you think there will be a way, Father?"

"To destroy the base?"

She nodded.

"I don't know."

"It seems so terrible to think that German submarines are constantly coming and going through our waters, using it as a base for destroying Allied ships, and... and we're unable to do a thing."

He turned his worn eyes from the water front to the hills. Gestapo sentries were roaming the hills. He turned his eyes once more to the fjord.

Borghild said, "It is impossible to hope of breaking, away from the town."

"I pray that no one will try. He would only be shot. And if he did escape... by some miracle... there would be reprisals, like we are hearing of from Poland, and France."

She wondered if her letter had not accomplished its purpose. Her cousin had answered, but there had been no indication that she had understood, that she had learned the secret. And she had written to her cousin, but she had never dared again to try what she had done. Perhaps, she sometimes thought, it might be best if her plan did not work. And yet...

Her father was saying, "I've wondered if God intends for us to remain in subjection. Perhaps it is best that way... for our faith."

Hot thrusts, chill pricks, shot through Borghild's spine. If there were an extended occupation, years, perhaps, it would mean months of dodging Schreckenbach, months of shunning the night, avoiding seclusions, for fear of meeting him... alone.

"Do... you really think so, Father?"

"It isn't a pleasant thought."

"Will... will England fall?"

"I pray not!"

"Surely Hitler's armies can't cross the English, Channel? Can they? No one has before?"

"There are many things never done before... which have been done by the Nazis."

"Then—?"

He smiled, "But I am positive God will not let Great Britain, Europe's fortress of democracy, fall!"

Borghild beamed. "You think England will—"

He challenged her optimism, "But it may be a long battle."

"Oh."

"And as long as it lasts, it is probable that we shall be bound," his eyes sought the hills again, the scenic *bakke* where he longed to stroll, and, seeing a sentry, he finished, "bound by the horrible shackles of Nazism."

"We have been treated quite well, though."

"Yes... we have."

"There will be difficulties about the food."

He frowned. "When people are hungry, Borghild—"

"I understand."

"God can supply! ...And yet, He may ask us to suffer physical want, that the Nazis may see how robust our souls can be, though our bodies are hungry."

Sigurd, who had been trimming the hedge, approached.

"It's warm," his employer said.

"The heat bothers me," Sigurd growled, looking toward the fjord, "when my blood cooks after a look over there. Otherwise I wouldn't—"

"We must make the best of it."

He smiled. "I'm in fair humor though... I heard a couple of new jokes about the Nazis."

"Let's hear them," Prest Gran laughed.

"They say some Nazi soldiers got drunk in Bergen the other night. They got into a car and drove, like the drunken maniacs they were, down the street. The street they were on went right out to a pier, and because it was dark and the pier wasn't lighted, the Nazis drove out into the sea!" He released a typical chuckle. "The Gestapo hurried to the scene and questioned an old fisher woman at the end of the pier. 'Did you see the car coming?' they asked her. 'Yes, I did,' she told them. They swore at her and asked her, 'Why didn't you stop it?'" Another chuckle. "The old lady shrugged her shoulders and asked, 'Why should I? I thought they were on their way to England!'"

"Sigurd, where do—?"

"And then," he cut in, "they tell a story about a Nazi flier whose job it is to sit on the Eiffel Tower and look through binoculars until he sees the white flag raised over London. One of his friends asked him if it didn't get monotonous. 'Sure,' he admitted, 'but it's permanent.' I heard another—"

"Quiet, Sigurd!" Prest Gran whispered.

"Huh?"

Bruno Schreckenbach was approaching.

Boldly, pretending not to see the approaching Nan, Sigurd continued, "They tell of two Belgians who met—"

"Quiet, Sigurd!"

"Two Belgians," he ignored, "met on the street. They saluted each other, and said, 'Heil Rubens!' A Gestapo," he emphasized that word above his loud voice, "officer overheard and demanded an explanation. They said, 'Oh, we Belgians have a famous painter, too!' I've a notion that kept him quiet for a—"

"Heil Hitler!"

Sigurd turned, and sneered, "Heil Dahl!" naming the eminent Norwegian landscape painter.

"Sigurd!" Prest Gran gasped.

"Swine!" from Schreckenbach.

"Oh!" Borghild gasped. And again, "Oh!"

Schreckenbach smote her with his eyes.

"Say, Schreckenbach!" Sigurd giggled. "I heard the other day why you Nazis are anti-Semitic—"

"Sigurd!" Prest Gran shouted.

Schreckenbach's attention was centered on Borghild, though the quick twitch of his shoulders assured Sigurd that he heard.

Sigurd finished, "I hear you Nazis are persecuting the Jews, because you've got the idea that they still have the staff of Moses, and Hitler needs that staff, so he can cross the English Channel like the Israelites crossed the Red Sea!"

Schreckenbach turned to Sigurd. He cursed violently in German.

Borghild shook herself from the hypnotic spell cast by his eyes and rushed into the house.

"Was... is... was," Prest Gran searched his mind for words, "there something you... wanted?"

Bruno Schreckenbach took a step toward the door. Perhaps he heard the click of the latch as Borghild locked it. Anyway, he stopped.

The minister continued, "Our house has been checked for food."

"I was passing by," Schreckenbach said. "I'll go now."

"But—"

"Good day, sir."

He bowed and left.

"Hmph!" Sigurd snorted.

"Strange," Prest Gran frowned, perplexed.

Then, without comment, they watched Schreckenbach stomp away—like an enraged bull... or was it as a frustrated suitor?

"He came a few weeks ago," Prest Gran said, "one evening. He asked if I were home alone. I told him all had retired but I. He seemed to want to say something... and then, as bluntly as today, he left."

"Maybe," Sigurd suggested, "he's trying to get something over on us." He growled, "It's been a long time since his Gestapo rats had a good excuse for killing somebody!"

"I wouldn't say that, Sigurd. I... I'm praying that it is because he is burdened about his sins."

"Humph! That beast? He hasn't—"

"God's Word is quick, powerful, sharper than a two-edged sword, Sigurd! It will reveal sin to any man, however seared his conscience, if he gives heed to its message."

"Schreckenbach surely hasn't been giving heed, has he?"

"He has been coming to church."

"To be sure no anti-Nazi plans are laid!"

"He has listened attentively to the preaching, Sigurd."

"To catch you at your words, like those Pharisees did to Christ!"

"I know men quite well, Sigurd. I see a man's soul... mirrored on his face. I—"

Borghild opened the door, whispered, "Has he gone?" "Yes."

She came out. "The presence of that man frightens me!"

Sigurd said, "You can be glad Hans Laub doesn't come. He makes Schreckenbach as tame as a kitten!"

The parent asked, "Why do you suppose he came, Borghild?"

"To see—" She bit her tongue, slicing the sentence before it could betray her thoughts. "Wh-Why do you think he came?"

"I don't know."

"Did... didn't he say... anything?"

Prest Gran shook his head. "Only that he was passing by, and that he was going again."

"He is strange."

"Very strange," her father admitted.

In the secluded shadows of a great birch, Bruno Schreckenbach paused to look back. He wanted to return, to break through the door in the name of the Gestapo, and compel Borghild Gran to come with him. But he loved her, and he could not take her by violence so long as there was the faintest hope of winning her legitimately.

He saw when she returned to the veranda. She was beautiful as she stood speaking to her father. Surely, he thought, the master race must include Norse blood, for he had never seen a champion to her beauty.

With his imagination, he destroyed the distance between them. She was in his arms... as she had been those few moments of that night in the cemetery. That night! If he marched triumphantly with Herr Hitler across the Thames River, but never had her in his arms again, that night he held her to him would subordinate the day of victory! He would spend his life-long quests for happiness on thoughts of that night... if he should be denied her. But he would not be denied her! He must have her! She must be his! She must be!

He took a step toward returning to her, but she was looking toward his hiding place, and if she saw him emerge from it, he knew she would return to the house.

So, hopeful of a better future, he turned his steps toward the hotel.

In his suite, Hans Laub was again giving audience to Leif Hunseid.

"Yes, Leif, it even surprises me how successful things have gone for us here. Resistance has been negligible! Our sentries have set up an impregnable wall outside the town! Enough to make the Führer himself take time to smile, eh?" Through his window, he could see the fjord. "Excellent camouflage, too. Excellent! The British have been recruiting colorblind men, you know, because they can detect camouflage from the air. But not our kind, eh, Leif?"

Hunseid laughed, "Not a chance!"

"Yes, sir, Leif, I expect to come before the Reichstag some day and report the finest example of Nazi technique of the entire Norwegian campaign. And you'll be with me, Leif! You'll be with me! Unless," he laughed, "we can go through the war without these Norwegians knowing what a," he winked, "crook you are, and you decide to remain here, as a fine Norwegian citizen. I marvel at you,

Leif, really I do. You were the only Quisling man in town, but you handled the work expertly."

"There wasn't much to it, Hans."

"Modesty isn't a Nazi virtue, Leif! You can be proud of yourself!"

There was tapping at his door.

"Must be Bruno," Hans Laub whispered. "You, Bruno?" he called.

"Yes."

"Come in."

Bruno Schreckenbach entered.

"Well," Laub asked, "why so dejected, Bruno?"

"I am very tired."

"Tired? Don't try to fool me, Bruno. It has something to do with the Gran girl, doesn't it?"

"Umh... uh..."

"You're a card, Bruno!"

"Cupid got you with one shot!" Hunseid added.

"It isn't funny!" Bruno Schreckenbach's face turned crimson. "I love that girl!" He cursed. "You two have never thought of women in terms of love... real love... like I do Miss Gran! But I can't win her! She evades me! It isn't funny!"

Fat Laub trembled with laughter, and his profuse stomach swayed, like a soap bubble about to burst in the wind.

Leif Hunseid coughed. Laughter had sent a swallow of saliva on the wrong route.

"It isn't funny, I tell you! It isn't funny! It wouldn't surprise me much if you won't keep your promise after the war is over. There'll be a peace treaty that will forbid me to take her back to Germany against her will, so I can teach her to love me! And then you'll laugh! You'll laugh! I tell you, I love that woman!"

"Bruno!" Hans Laub held a restraining hand to the disgruntled suitor. "Do you doubt my word, Bruno? Do you—?"

"I love her, I tell you!"

"Swine! Did we say you couldn't love her, if you wanted to?" Laub barked. "Of course you'll take her with you to Germany!

When this Norwegian lover of hers is out of the way, she'll want somebody! It might as well be you!"

"But—"

"Do you want her kidnapped," he whispered, "and kept prisoner here in the hotel?"

"I'm sorry, Hans," Schreckenbach lowered his voice. "I was a bit hasty. The girl infatuates me so. I'm sorry. I'll be more patient."

"There now," Laub smiled, "that's better." He frowned, "For a moment, I was afraid you were putting personal interests ahead of the program of the Third Reich. But you wouldn't do that... would you?"

"N-No. Certainly not."

"Good! I'm really pleased with your work, Bruno. ' Very pleased! Your sentries have done amazingly fine work!"

"Yes, Bruno," Hunseid said, "very fine!"

"Look out on the fjord, men," Hans Laub gloated, pointing to the water. "See, the Norwegians are going ' home from their work. They don't know that the U-boats docked there now are five of the very best Germany has! The British don't know either!"

It was rapidly growing dusk, now, and the camouflage was more impressive than in the daytime. To anyone who did not know, the Bjerkely water front was no more than an ordinary Norwegian fishing port.

"A sight to see, isn't it, men?" Laub boasted.

"A sight to see!"

"Yes," Schreckenbach grunted.

"I think," Laub continued, "that when the war is over, we'll have to let the British in on our secret, won't we? We'll take Churchill and King George on a little excursion! I'd like to personally show them this U-boat base, I—" He stopped short, to ask, "I didn't hear planes?" He stepped closer to the window. "Sounds like quite a formation, flying low." Looking through the window, he cursed and shouted, "Men, look! R. A. F. bombers! A dozen of them! They—"

But that was all he had time to say. The first member of the formation swooped over the water front. There was a brief whistling, as four bombs dropped through the thousand feet of space between the plane and the U-boat base!

And then the explosion! It was terrific! Great slabs of concrete flew into the air and dropped into the fjord! Water sprayed over the town, as though there were a cloudburst! Windows shook under the impact! Some were broken!

And then the next plane, and the next, and the next! Their tons of explosives blew the base to bits, churned the fjord into a lather, shook the town like an earthquake! The frame buildings—the excellent camouflage—had disappeared! The batteries were twisted and thrown from their concrete foundations!

The three men in the hotel cursed like a demon chorus of hell! In their fury they struck each other, kicked the furniture, tore their clothes!

When the last British plane was heading out to sea, and the populace could be seen running, wide-eyed, to the fjord, Hans Laub shrieked, "Do something, Bruno! Take some of the men captive! Tell the people they'll be shot tomorrow unless the one who revealed our secret to the British is found! Don't stand there, Bruno! You fool! You swine! Do something!"

"You do something!" Schreckenbach cursed.

"What can we do?" Hunseid wept, his hands drooping at his sides, his face transparent.

"Bruno!" Laub grabbed a revolver from his desk. "Come! We've got to do something! Come! Come!" Hysterically he shouted, "Come!"

They stumbled to the lobby and out into the street.

"Get your men together, Bruno! Round up a dozen of the finest Norwegian men! Do you hear me?"

"I hear you!" Schreckenbach cursed. "I hear you!"

Borghild had not gone with Bjarne, Sigurd, Birgit and her father to the scene of the bombing. She waited behind and watched through the shattered windows of their house.

She had expected the bombing soon, for in the mail, she had received a letter. It was in her hand as she watched, in her trembling hand.

It was from her cousin. It said:

Dearest Borghild,

When I got your letter of a few weeks ago, with the commemorative on it, I merely tore off that corner of the envelope and then put the stamp with my duplicates. But today, going over my duplicates, I prepared them for mounting, or trading, with other collectors. You perhaps remembered that Lars removed used stamps from the envelope paper by soaking them in water. That is the procedure I use, too, and I can assure you that the commemorative came off splendidly, in excellent condition.

Greet your—

But the rest of the letter does not matter. It was the fact that Kisa, her cousin, had taken the commemorative from the envelope paper... that she had soaked it in water, so that it came off without being torn.

Underneath that commemorative stamp, she had printed, with permanent ink, this message:

Kisa: Get word to British. Our fishing docks are camouflaged submarine base. Must be bombed! Please!

"Thank You, Lord!" she praised. "Thank You! The message got through! Thank you, Lord!"

Borghild watched from the Window, entranced. She did not leave the Window until Bjarne and her father returned.

"Sweetheart!" Bjarne exclaimed, coming to her. "Weren't you at the fjord?"

"N-No. I was... afraid."

"Schreckenbach has taken a dozen men into custody! They are to be shot tomorrow, unless the one who got the information to the R. A. F. confesses!"

"No, Bjarne!" she shrieked.

"Merciful God!" her father pleaded heavenward. "Merciful God!"

Borghild slumped into Bjarne's arms.

Sixteen

THERE WAS NO SLEEP in Bjerkely. There were lights in every house. Men and women were talking, praying. Children and babies lay awake in their beds and cribs. Next of kin to the twelve in custody paced their floors.

Borghild did not go to her room until three o'clock in the morning, when she left her father and Bjarne and Sigurd downstairs. She had to be alone, where she could think, and pray.

Did she do wrong? Should she not have sent the secret message to Stockholm? She had only done what she knew was the prayer of every true Bjerkely citizen. But was it wrong? She felt she had done right, and yet... Would the twelve men taken in custody die, if she did not confess that it was she who had sent the message? And if she did confess?

"Oh, God," she dropped to her knees, "guide me! Guide me, Lord God, guide me!"

A strange peace came to her, and until the first break of dawn, she slept.

Bruno Schreckenbach did not sleep. He did not retire. But, in the darkness of his room, he sat... not as a proud member of the conqueror's horde—or were they conquerors any longer?—but as a condemned man in death row at Moabit.

He was afraid to turn on the light, afraid that there was an enraged Norwegian in the tall birch outside his window; the British might have dropped guns, and the Norwegian might be waiting for him to turn on his light, revealing himself as a target.

He crept to the window. Like the murderer in Poe's Tale of the Telltale Heart, he thought his pounding heart was the footsteps of the enemy. He was certain he saw somebody below in the shadows... somebody looking up at him... waiting for him to turn on his light... waiting for revenge. Was it a parent? a brother? a woman, the wife, mother, or sweetheart of one of the men taken into custody?

"Who goes there?" he called, quickly ducking beneath the sill.

There was no answer.

Slowly, he took his gun from the holster, raised to the window, pointed the revolver at the shadows.

Foolishness! No one was there! It was his imagination!

He heard a twig snap! Sweat made swamps at his temples, rivers on his face. Without aiming, he fired into the shadows!

A frightened dog yelped and scampered away, leaving behind him his late supper of bone. Schreckenbach felt very foolish... and very relieved.

"Bruno!" It was Hans Laub, shrieking. "What was that?"

Schreckenbach turned on his light and stepped out into the hall.

"Bruno!" Laub repeated. "What was that?"

"There was somebody beneath my window," he said, "and I shot."

"A Norwegian?"

"Y-Yes."

"Did you—?"

"I'm sure I missed, Hans. He ran away. I don't think he was hurt."

Laub swore. "I'm not used to this!"

"I, either."

It pleased Schreckenbach somewhat to see the uneasiness on Laub's face. He walked to the engineer, and together they went to his suite.

Hans Laub spent fifteen seconds cursing, before he said, "Our project! Ruined! And five U-boats! Blown to bits! The Führer may send us to a concentration camp for this... he may have us shot!"

"But—"

"How did the Norwegians know, Bruno? There was not a Norwegian man who was near enough to be injured! I heard some boasting of that!"

"It isn't our fault, Hans. As for the men, all were off duty."

"Not our fault? Herr Hitler isn't a sympathetic mother! To him every error has a reason! We've failed, Bruno, failed miserably! It may cost us a great price!"

"But how did the British learn our secret? No one has left Bjerkely! All mail has been censored?"

"Perhaps there is a short wave transmitter hidden in the town."

"But our technicians in Oslo have constantly combed the ether waves for any enemy broadcast originating in Nor—"

"Maybe," Laub suggested, "someone threw a bottle out to sea."

"That couldn't—"

Hans Laub shouted, "Maybe Prest Gran threw it, with a prayer! I hate the prayers of these people, Bruno! I hate their prayers!"

This silenced Schreckenbach.

"We won't send a dispatch to Berlin, until our reprisal threats have brought a confession." He brightened, "We might send the guilty one back to Berlin, to be tried there in the presence of Hitler! That might make it easier for us!"

A knock at the door nearly caused Laub to lurch from his chair. "Who?"

"Roehm," one of Laub's secretaries answered from outside.

"Come."

"You asked for no dispatches to Berlin," the secretary squirmed, eying Laub as a tormented mouse does a cat, "but—"

Laub's cursing would have drowned the booming of a howitzer battery.

"Did you send a dispatch?"

"I—"

"Did you? If you did, I'll have you shot! I told you to wait!"

"Herr Laub!" Roehm pleaded.

"Kill him, Bruno! Kill him! Bruno! Kill him!"

"Herr Laub, I didn't send a dispatch!"

"Then why—?" Hans Laub cooled a bit.

"I came to tell you that we overheard a British broadcast downstairs! They describe the raid in detail! They name Bjerkely!"

"Roehm!" Hans Laub bellowed. "If you lie...!"

"It's the truth! I swear it!"

Schreckenbach asked, "Did they reveal how they got the information?"

"The news reporter only said it was given to them very cleverly."

"Was that all he said?" Laub demanded.

Roehm answered, "He laughed and said Sherlock Holmes himself couldn't trace the source, and, of course, the Gestapo never could."

"Bruno!" 'Laub half whined, half wept. "Berlin will hear! Berlin knows the base at Bjerkely has been destroyed! Bruno! Bruno!" He clawed his hair. "Bruno!"

Schreckenbach and Roehm left the mad man to his frenzy. Schreckenbach returned to his room, Roehm to the lobby.

Through the window of his unlighted room, Schreckenbach saw the lights of the town, flickering in every home, suggesting hatred, defiance, to him! Below he heard the squeaking boots of six of his men on patrol. That made him breathe more easily. But in the distance, faintly shimmering in the night light, lay the fjord. He was glad it was night, so that he could not see the destruction of the R. A. F. bombing. For a moment everything seemed unreal and he expected to awaken from a dream and find himself in Dahlem, ready for the day's work in the factory where he had wOrked before joining the Nazi Party, subsequent to becoming a member of the Gestapo.

And then, again, he knew that all was real.

The night was passing swiftly. It would soon be morning. The thought clutched at him! Morning! Laub, in his rage, would demand the execution of the twelve prisoners. And that atrocity would, perhaps, drive the girl he loved farther from his heart!

But that was not all. He could hear Prest Gran's quotation from the Bible, Thou shalt not kill. He remembered the many sermons, the challenges to the

Christian life, the admonishings that warned of the future to those who rejected Jesus Christ.

It was warm. He was sweaty. But a chill shook him, and he buttoned his shirt at the neck.

Borghild awakened at dawn. She arose, dressed, descended the stairs. Her father was in his study. The door to his study was open.

"You've been up all night, Father?"

He smiled and nodded.

"Aren't you terribly tired?"

"I couldn't sleep," he said. "I rest in the Lord. That is all the relaxation I can find now."

The agony on his face struck at her. What would he say, if he knew it was she who had been the reason for the bombing? Would he be angry? She was sure he would be proud of her. Yet she did not dare to tell him.

"Do you think the men will be shot, Father?" Her voice wavered.

For the moment it took him to say, "They are all believers in Christ," he smiled. Then he frowned, "I dread to see them go. I dread it!"

"Oh, Father, is there nothing we can do?"

"Pray... and be content with the answer."

She tried to smile. It was a poor attempt.

"I wonder," he said, "if it would help for me to go to the hotel and see Schreckenbach and Laub, and plead mercy for the men."

"Do... Do you think it might help, Father?"

"It is worth trying," he said, as he stood.

"Oh, Father, if only the men might be spared! Ragnvald is one of the men; he has four children! Gulbrand's mother is an invalid! Gunnar—"

"I will go now," he said.

"But—"

"Even now may be too late." He walked to the hall, took his hat from the shelf there.

"I will pray, Father! I will pray!"

"God bless you, dear girl!"

He left the house.

"Oh, God," she prayed, pacing the floor, "Thy will be done! Please, God! Please! Please!"

Bjarne descended the stairs.

"Have you slept?" she asked.

"In a subconscious stupor, and only a moment of that."

"It's horrible."

"Worse than that. Where is your father?"

"He has gone to the hotel."

"The hotel?" he exclaimed.

"To plead mercy for the men."

"Mercy? From Laub and Schreckenbach?"

"Father will approach them as an ambassador of heaven." She threw her arms around Bjarne. "Oh, Bjarne, they will listen to Father, won't they?"

"I... I hope so." He placed his arms about her. "Dear Borghild, this is no life for a woman." He whispered, "If it would have been possible to arrange for a license, we would have been married weeks ago."

She turned her tear-streaked face to his. Their lips met, tenderly, and Without haste.

"I love you," she whispered. "I love you so much."

"Maybe," his voice was as muffled as hers had been, "there will be a chance to escape. If there is, we will be married."

"Married!" she screamed. And for a rapturous moment, as they kissed again, both forgot everything but their love.

Prest Gran pushed the doorbell button firmly. It was Laub's secretary, Roehm, who came to the door. The fearful lines on Roehm's face, the way he trembled when he spoke, encouraged the minister.

"What do you want?"

"May I see Hans Laub?... or Bruno Schreckenbach?"

"You are Prest Gran?"

"Yes."

"I will see."

He shut the door. Prest Gran heard it lock. In a minute, he returned.

"You may come, Herr Laub says, if you come alone."

"I am alone."

"Come."

"Thank you."

Roehm led the way to Laub's door. "In here," he said, and pushed it open. Then he left.

Hans Laub stood. "Have you the name of the guilty one?"

Bruno Schreckenbach was a pace behind Laub.

"N-No. I came to ask you to be merciful to the—"

"Merciful?" Hans Laub growled. "You ask for mercy, when your people have helped the British to destroy our base? You have delayed the deliverance of Europe! You have spit in the face of the Führer! You have—"

"I have come in the Name of Christ," Prest Gran said simply.

Laub glared. Schreckenbach's eyes focused on the floor.

"Each of those men has his faith in Jesus Christ. It is dangerous for you to harm them. I warn you."

"None of that! Jesus Christ! A fanatical Jew... if He ever lived at all!"

"He was the Son of God," Prest Gran said, "He is God, the Son. He loves all men. He would have them to look unto Him and be saved."

"Rot! If you haven't the identity of the guilty person, then please don't waste my time! I am busy!"

"But—"

"I am busy!"

"You aren't going to have those men killed, are you?"

"Of course I am! In less than an hour... unless a confession is made!"

"But what good will it do?"

"It will teach the people of Bjerkely a lesson! It will give me revenge!" He looked through the window toward the fjord. "It will show them how angry I am for what has been done!"

"I have been begging my people to be patient. The Norwegians are fair to all men. But when they lose their patience—"

"They have no guns."

"But if there were a riot, they outnumber you and your men at least twenty to one."

Laub's eyes narrowed. "Are you hinting that there is a riot brewing?"

"I am not hinting. I have only read men's faces. You can chain dogs, Mr. Laub, but you can't shackle men unjustly. Justice is inevitable. Be reasonable... to us and to yourself! Promise me the men will be unharmed!"

"Nonsense!"

"It will do no good!" Prest Gran insisted.

"Perhaps," Laub sneered, "the first mass execution will be wasted lives... but when Herr Schreckenbach selects twenty-four men to be killed, unless the guilty man confesses—"

"No! I beg you! Have you no heart?"

'It must be done, Prest Gran."

"God's Word, says, Thou shalt not kill. It warns that murderers shall have their part in the lake which burneth with fire and brimstone. You challenge God if you kill those men! I warn you!"

Pale Schreckenbach trembled. "Perhaps—" he began to suggest to Laub.

"Shut up! Are you a woman?"

"Listen to him," Prest Gran urged. "But don't murder those men! I beg you! They have wives, children, mothers, fathers! Please!"

"Is there no other way, Hans?" Schreckenbach asked Laub in German.

"Spare them!" Prest Gran continued. "Don't shoot them! I beg you! Don't shoot them!"

There was a moment of silence. Then Hans Laub said, very slowly, "You may go, Prest Gran... with my promise that the men will not be shot."

Schreckenbach jolted with suppressed delight.

Prest Gran exclaimed, "You are telling me the truth?"

"I have given you my word," Laub said as slowly as before. "The men will not be shot."

"Thank you, sir! Thank you!"

With tears in his eyes, Prest Gran turned and left.

He hurried toward the *Prestegaarden*. A dozen stopped him, and he shared the good news with them. They danced into their homes, or down the streets, to share the news with others.

He rushed into his house. "Thank God!" he shouted. "Laub gave me his word the men wouldn't be, shot!"

"Father!" Borghild, pulling Bjarne by the hand, ran to him. "Have the men been released?"

"N-No, but I'm sure they shall."

"You saw Laub himself?" Bjarne asked.

"In the hotel."

"I didn't know he had any heart."

"I'm so thankful!"

"It's wonderful!" Borghild cried.

"But," Bjarne was still a pessimist, "won't he take any action to punish us for the bombing of the base?" He continued in the same breath, "It's worth a lot knowing that place has been destroyed! And the front is so ruined, there isn't a chance of rebuilding!"

"I'm so happy I could cry!" Borghild shouted.

And then she did cry.

Bjarne pillowed her head against his chest. Prest Gran placed his arms about both of them.

"It may be difficult, my children, but God is with us! He will never leave us nor forsake us! His eye is on the sparrow! The hairs of our heads are numbered! He know? He knows!"

There was silence, for there was no need of words.

When they stood separately, Bjarne said, "Maybe the British will make another move. The fjord is heavily patrolled, but I have heard of supplies being dropped by parachute. If we had guns and ammunition, we could drive the Nazis from Bjerkely!"

"No, Bjarne. Norway is in Nazi hands. Our uprising would soon be put down... with much loss of life, perhaps."

"Perhaps," Bjarne admitted.

Borghild, thrilled to think that she was not to be the cause of the men's death, said, "I'm not in the mood for dark thoughts. Let's talk about the brighter side of things." Her eyes twinkled with morning light. "Shall I have my mother's wedding dress remodeled for me, Bjarne?"

"That's right!" Prest Gran smiled. "There'll be a wedding as soon as we can at least be as normal as the ' rest of Norway! I haven't performed a wedding in weeks, have I?" He chuckled, "Just in case I might be a trifle rusty, let me perform your ceremony next... so I won't be too embarrassed if I should make a few mistakes."

"We'll plan on that, Father!"

"Suits me fine!"

"You will found a wonderful home," Prest Gran said. "You have the love that endures, that mellows but never grOws cold. You have Christ to be the unseen Host of your house." He seemed a little lonesome, as he said, "I'm rapidly becoming an old man, but I have fond dreams of holding your children on my lap... as I used to hold you, Borghild... and Lars."

"You're wonderful, Father!"

Bjarne quickened the pace of his eyes.

"Life is brief," the father continued. "It is but the prelude to eternity. Yet, among all the cares and disappointments, God gives us many pleasant things."

Bjarne put one arm about Borghild's waist. She did the same to him.

"It always thrills me that, of all human affections, Christ chose to illustrate His love to the Church by speaking of the Church as His bride, and of Himself as the Bridegroom"

Bjarne tightened the arm about her waist. She did the same to him.

"One can never fully understand the love of Christ, with what understanding human mind is capable of, until he has known the marital love of a devoted mate."

His eyes turned to a portrait of his wife. And then they turned away, moist.

"We will be very happy," Borghild whispered. "Bjarne is the dearest man in all the world to me. I love him so!"

"God bless you, my children!"

There was another long silence.

Prest Gran broke that silence, asking, "Have you seen Birgit? It's about time for breakfast, isn't it?"

"I know I'm hungry," Bjarne said.

"I'll go to the kitchen," Borghild said, "and see if—"

The door flew open. Sigurd burst in. His eyes were wide. He was pale. He trembled.

"Sigurd!" Prest Gran asked. "What's wrong?"

"The men!" Sigurd gasped.

"The twelve?" Prest Gran demanded.

Bjarne shouted, "They haven't been shot, have they?"

Prest Gran exclaimed, "No! Hans Laub promised me—"

"Not shot!" Sigurd panted. "They're hanging by the neck from the trees in the square!"

"Merciful God! Merciful God!"

Bjarne was silent, staring.

Borghild made a desperate effort, but she would have fallen to the floor if Bjarne had not caught her as she collapsed.

Seventeen

IT WAS MIDMORNING before Prest Gran came from his study, Bjarne broke the spell. that kept his eyes staring at the floor, and Borghild spoke.

"I'm glad the men were Christians," she mumbled, for that was her only comfort—when she thought of the headless homes, the widows, the fatherless children, the heartbroken sweethearts.

"Yes," Prest Gran said, "for them all is well," and in subdued tones, he added, "At times I am envious."

"But this probably isn't the end," Bjarne sighed.

"No," from Prest Gran. "Hans Laub implied that he will double the hostages who are to be killed, until the guilty one confesses."

Deep breaths fortified Borghild's capsizing equilibrium.

"Rat!" Bjarne fumed. "Promised you the men wouldn't be shot... and then had them hung! That's a Nazi! If the world falls beneath the swastika—"

"No, Bjarne!" Prest Gran interrupted. "You forget the Prince of Peace! Perhaps the time of our redemption draweth nigh!" He turned his face upward, and, for a moment, it resembled the artist's portrayal of the Master in Gethsemane. "Even so, come, Lord Jesus!"

"Father, do you think more will be held hostage?"

"I—"

Bjarne suggested, "Wouldn't it help for us to go and see Laub? If he'll be patient, the guilty one will confess."

Borghild steadied herself.

"Don't you think so?" Bjarne asked her. "I say, don't you think so, Borghild?"

"Yes... Yes, certainly."

"Come, Bjarne," Prest Gran urged "We'll go to the hotel."

"Father! Maybe—"

"We must make every effort... at any risk. Come, Bjarne."

"Yes, I'll go with you." To Borghild he assured, "We'll be safe, dear. Don't worry."

"I...I..."

"We won't be long."

They left.

Borghild stood at the window and watched them go. What if they knew the truth? What if they knew it was she? Would they be proud? Or... A mother passed by, holding the hand of her young son. She cast quick glances at the house. Did people suspect? Would she be Bjerkely's heroine... or Bjerkely's traitor... if people knew?

She went to the living room, opened her Bible. It opened at the sixty-ninth Psalm.

> Save me, O God; for the waters are come in unto my soul.
>
> I sink in deep mire, where there is no standing: I am come into deep waters, Where the floods overflow me.
>
> I am weary of m crying: my throat is dried: mine eyes fail while I wait for my God.
>
> They that hate me without a cause are more than the hairs of mine head: they that would destroy me, being mine enemies wrongfully, are mighty: then I restored that which I took not away.
>
> O God, thou knowest my foolishness; and my sins are not hid from thee.

Let not them that wait on thee, O Lord God of hosts, be ashamed for my sake: let not those that seek thee be confounded for my sake, O God of Israel.

Because for thy sake I have borne reproach; shame hath covered my face.

I am become a stranger unto my brethren, and an alien unto my—

No! This could not mean her! She was not an Achan in the camp! She had done what any Bjerkely citizen would have done, had he had the same opportunity as she! And had someone else betrayed the Nazis, she would have been glad to die as a hostage! Glad to die? If she surrendered... confessed... would she have to die? Die! Would she have to die?

"Oh, God!" She sobbed. "I'm not afraid to die, but—! Oh, God! Oh, merciful God! Please show me what to do! Please, Lord God, please!"

Prest Gran and Bjarne met many of the townspeople between the *Prestegaarden* and Leif Hunseid's hotel. Above their sullen steps, they saw the anger, which had displaced astonishment, in their eyes. Prest Gran greeted each cordially. And when such a one was met, he offered sympathy, condolence and hope.

On an untrodden shortcut, he said to Bjarne, "These are wonderful people. There are none better. I have never known a town to have so many saints." And then the glow in his eye, the bell-like tone of his voice, changed. "But even the loving Saviour exercised wrath when He drove out the money changers."

"You mean—?"

"It is not wrong to fight for justice. I am not a pacifist. I have tried to keep the people patient... while we waited. But now..."

"I understand what you mean."

"There will be much trouble if the Nazis take more hostages."

"Revolt?"

"I fear it, Bjarne."

"But the Nazis have guns. We are disarmed."

"There would be great loss of life. But if I know Bjerkely men, they would rather chose their deaths than die as Hans Laub and Schreckenbach choose."

"It would be massacre."

"It would, Bjarne... but I fear it. An animal accustomed to the open spaces becomes restless in his cage. Free men are that way. Animals don't know how to plan strategy; but free men do."

"If we could storm one of the sentries," Bjarne proposed, "and get his guns and ammunition—"

"See, Bjarne! You are planning! It is spontaneous!"

"I... I guess it is!" Bjarne admitted, seeing within himself the desire of all Bjerkely... the price that he, like all Bjerkely, was willing to pay for the accomplishment of that desire.

"When a man has been free, and is enslaved, he becomes mad to regain his freedom. Slaves who have been bound since birth can be content. But not free men."

Ahead of them, Leif Hunseid and Bruno Schreckenbach were in Hans Laub's suite at the hotel.

On Laub's desk was a dispatch which had arrived a few moments before. It read:

> Hans Laub
> Bjerkely Project
> Norway
>
> Why have we not received reports? British propaganda broadcast boasts of bombing at your location. Send statement immediately.

Office of the Führer

"What am I going to do, men?" Laub pleaded.

"It isn't your fault," Hunseid tried to comfort.

Hans Laub cursed. "I don't need sympathy! I need a solution!" He reread the message from Berlin. "What shall I answer? Shall I deny the bombing? Shall I..." He cursed again. "Don't stand there and gawk at me like a Jew and a Pole! Tell me what to do!"

Schreckenbach said, "Send a message to Berlin. They will listen to reason. Goering isn't shot because a big Dornier goes down in the Channel. Battles may be lost without losing the war. Why—"

"Shut up, Schreckenbach! Dunce! I want to know what—"

Hunseid interrupted, "I think he's right, Hans. Send an explanation to Berlin. Explain what happened, and that we're doing everything we can to convict the guilty one."

"You're proud," Schreckenbach sneered, "too proud to report that your pet project has—"

"Schreckenbach! That made me mad enough to crush you with my hands!"

Bruno Schreckenbach, like a spunky dog, took an offensive step toward Hans Laub.

"Don't be fools, men. We've got to listen to reason." Hunseid mediated. "Wars are lost, you know, when a nation stops fighting the enemy to fight Within itself. If ever you two needed to cooperate, it's now!"

"Sorry," Schreckenbach whined.

Hans Laub only glared, submissively.

"The damage is done, Hans," Leif Hunseid continued. "and nothing we can do will repair it. The only thing to do now is to take more hostages, kill more hostages if necessary, until we find the traitor."

There was tapping at the door.

"Who?"

"Roehm."

"Come in!" Laub snapped. When his secretary entered, he added, "But be quick!"

"Prest Gran wishes to see you."

Laub cursed. "What does he want, the prattling old religionist... to save my soul from the hell he preaches all of us Nazis into?"

"He didn't say," Roehm answered. "He only said he wanted to see you."

"You may be able to make him your tool, Hans," Hunseid suggested. "He will do much to save his people misery."

"Hmmm." Laub asked his secretary, "Is he alone?"

"The man who stays at his house is with him."

"The old fool?"

"The young man."

Schreckenbach stiffened.

"Tell Gran he may come... if he comes alone. Hard telling what that young fellow—"

"Let him come too, Hans," Schreckenbach suggested with noticeable eagerness.

"Why?"

"What harm can he do?"

"Let them both come then," Laub swore. "What would it matter if they threw a grenade into the room and ran?"

"Perhaps," Leif Hunseid hesitated, "I had better go. ,I—I am a faithful one, you know."

"Maybe you'd better," Schreckenbach said.

Hunseid turned to leave. Then he said, "Wait a minute! I'll be here, pretending to plead for the lives of the people!"

"Good idea," Laub mumbled, with only a tinge of enthusiasm.

Hunseid cleared his throat. "Have mercy, Laub, I beg you! Haven't you a heart—?"

"Shut up! What ails you!"

"I'm playing my part, Hans," Hunseid whispered. "Don't you get it?"

"Go ahead."

Again Leif Hunseid cleared his throat. He could act at pantomime, but he Was very poor at dialogue. "How can you take the lives of innocent people? What had those twelve men done? I tell you, it's brutal! As mayor of Bjerkely, I demand—"

There was tapping at the door again. '

"Prest Gran," Roehm announced.

"Come," Laub invited.

Leif Hunseid whimpered, "God has sent you, Prest Gran! I've been pleading for our people! Can you help me?"

It took a moment for him to say, "My heart is heavy for the people. They are great folk... none better in the world."

No one noticed that Bruno Schreckenbach had edged six inches closer to the door.

"Well, Prest Gran," Laub snapped, "what is it you want?"

"I hardly need to state my purpose, do I?"

"If you wish to make it known to me, you do!"

"Very well. As pastor of God's flock in Bjerkely, I—"

"Oh, that sickens me!" Laub burst. "What's your reason for calling?"

Bruno Schreckenbach was at the door, slowly opening it.

Prest Gran continued, "I must make it emphatic, sir, that as a servant of God, I come demanding justice. Unless you are a beast, your conscience has told you continually, since the first death you caused here, how unjust things are. God will not—"

"Gran! I am godless! I accept the philosophy of my comrade, Karl Marx, 'Religion is the opiate of the people.' Power goes with me! Religion is for the weaklings!"

Prest Gran quoted from the Psalms, "The fool hath said in his heart, There is no God."

"Have you come to preach?"

Bruno Schreckenbach was gone.

Prest Gran assumed every inch of his height. "Then I shall approach you with common sense reasoning! Believe me, What I shall say is for your own good! Bjerkely is disarmed. But free men will fight as long as they have arms and legs. Don't misunderstand me. I am not organizing my people to fight. But I can read men's faces. I see forebodings."

"Foolishness! What can they do?"

"Perhaps you have never seen what free men will do when they have been enslaved."

"Well, what do you suggest?"

Prest Gran paused before he continued. "I am not asking any promises from you." He forced Laub to turn aside his eyes. "You have proved to me how you keep promises. Be reasonable, for your own sake. Give the people time. The one who gave the information will confess, if he is in Bjerkely."

"What do you mean, if he is in Bjerkely?"

"Isn't it possible," Prest Gran suggested, "that British spies may have tapped your telephone lines, or intercepted a dispatch concerning your submarine base here?"

"Impossible!"

"Is it any more unreasonable to suggest something like that, than to think the information was sent from here, when your vigilance has been so strict?"

Laub only grunted.

"Be merciful," Hunseid begged. "Why should you hate us Norwegians so?"

To Hunseid's delight, Laub played his role. He pointed to the fjord, and asked, "Are you blind, Hunseid?"

"But we didn't ask you to come and build the base."

"Hunseid, you Norwegians will never understand, will you? Of course, you didn't ask us to come! We had to come! When the R. A. F. bombed here, they were bombing Norway every bit as much as they were bombing German property!"

"But," Hunseid said, "you notice how careful the British bombardiers were not to injure any of the town property."

"Hunseid!" Laub swore. "Maybe you are the one Who betrayed to the British the information!"

"No!" the Quislinger defied. "How could I?"

Prest Gran interrupted, addressing Laub, "I must go. Please think seriously of What I have said."

Hans Laub grinned, "If I see any advantage... yes."

"Come, Bjarne, we will go."

They left.

Outside, Bjarne said, "Hunseid put on a great front, didn't he?"

"I should be amused... but it is too tragic. He has been a native for years, but always, unknown to us, a traitor."

"And we're the only ones who know it," Bjarne said. "Hunseid has been whispering around town, trying to find out who sent the news to the British, so he could protect whoever did it. I'm afraid the guilty one may confide in him, and then..."

"Perhaps we should make our information known, Bjarne."

"And be shot? Besides, the people wouldn't believe us."

"You are right," Prest Gran said. "Sometimes, though, I find myself resigned to such extremes." He sighed, "God knows how anxious I am to be taken Home... if He is through with me here."

"No!" Bjarne objected. "You have much work yet!"

"Perhaps, Bjarne, perhaps. Are you in a hurry to get home?"

"N-No, why?"

"I feel the need to go to the church... to pray."

"I'll be glad to go with you. Have you the keys?"

"Yes."

When he had left Hans Laub's suite unobserved, Bruno Schreckenbach quickened his pace, its momentum increasing as he neared the *Prestegaarden*.

He suspected that Borghild would peep through the window on the door, before opening to give admittance; so after he had sounded the door chimes, he stepped to one side, out of sight.

The door opened. He stepped to it quickly.

"Oh," Borghild gasped, "it's you!"

"I had to come, Miss Gran!"

"I suppose you saw my father and Bjarne leave."

"Y-Yes, I did."

"You can't come in."

He placed his foot against the door. "Please."

"NO!"

"You need not be afraid."

"Afraid? Not afraid of a hangman? How brave should a woman be?"

"I can only be kind to you," he whispered. "Please let me come in."

But she was defiant, so, defying her, he pushed his way in.

"Stay out!" she begged.

But it was no use. He closed the door behind him.

"I must see you," he said.

She tried to be brave. "I didn't invite you; but what do you want?"

"I must tell you again that... that I... love you."

The words nauseated her, and her words lodged in her throat.

"How long will it be until you tell me you love me, too?"

She glared at him, laughed at him, and said, "Until east meets west!"

"Miss Gran!"

"How could I ever love... an executioner?"

"But... Miss Gran... I must do my duties to my country. Aren't you proud of Norway's warrior heroes?"

"Of her heroes, yes. But I have never been taught to admire Swain, the Viking, who murdered hundreds of Englishmen in the eighth century, after his men had killed the sheriff at Dorchester!"

He was silent.

"I am proud," she said firmly, "of defensive heroes who become aggressive! Do I make myself clear?"

"Miss Gran, I must tell you something." He fumbled with his hands, until she suspected a proposal. "Unless Hans Laub learns who betrayed our base to the British within the next hours, twenty-four more hostages will be taken. Bjarne Kolstad is to be one—"

"Bruno Schreckenbach! This is your work! You—"

He became violently brave. Grasping her with her arms, he shouted, "You have been promised to me, as part of the Victor's spoils! I will give my lifetime, after the war, to making you love me! Do you hear me?" He tried to kiss her, but she covered her mouth with her hands. "I am to have you! I am taking you back to Germany when the war is over! That will be soon! Then I shall have you!"

"Let me go! You're a brute! Let me go!"

"Will you talk to me," he said calmly, "if I let you go?"

"Anything."

He released her.

"But talk fast. You must go soon."

"I will go soon, Miss Gran. But first I have a proposition. If Bjarne Kolstad is spared, will you reward me with your love? Will you be—"

"Oh," she gasped, "you horrible thing!"

"I will make that bargain with you."

"Bargain! Robbery!"

"Miss Gran, can't you—"

"Bjarne would rather die than know that I would give my love to you! Something that is impossible... loving you!"

"But—"

"I pity you, Bruno Schreckenbach, when you stand before God's judgment seat! I pity you, and Hans Laub, and Adolf Hitler, and... and all the rest of you! You've defied God! You've murdered! You've killed women and children! You've broken homes! You've ruined cities! The Nazis are agents of hell! Agents of hell, I tell you!" She stopped for breath. "And you are one of them! Do you hear me? You are one of them!"

"Miss Gran, you—"

"You need to give your life to the Lord Jesus! You need to confess your horrible sins! If you would, you wouldn't be an executioner! You wouldn't rob children of their fathers! Wives of their husbands!" She gasped, "Women of their sweethearts!"

"You—"

"No one can really know what love is until he has known the love of God, the love that made a way of salvation so great you, or Hans Laub, or... or Adolf Hitler himself could be forgiven, if you would repent! But what does Christianity mean to you? The Cross conflicts with the principles of the swastika! The Bible condemns *Mein Kampf*! Christianity is counterclockwise to Nazism! Have you never known the ways of righteousness? Did you torture birds when you were a boy? Did you pull the wings off of flies? Did you—"

"I have known," he interrupted.

"Known? Known what?"

"The things of which you speak."

"Righteousness?"

He nodded.

She scoffed, "Were you ever inside a church before you came to Bjerkely?"

He nodded.

"A Jewish synagogue... to break up a service and send the rabbi and his people to a concentration camp?"

"I—"

"If you knew the first principles of righteousness, even if you do reject the saving blood of Christ, you couldn't be so brutal as you are! If you had had any Christian influence upon your life—"

"Miss Gran, listen to me!"

"More excuses! I'll listen."

"My home is Dahlem," he said, edging, nervously, to the door. "I... I regularly attended Dahlem Evangelical Church until I joined... the... the Nazi Party."

"Dahlem Evangelical Church!" she exclaimed, wide eyed.

"Yes," his eyes were downcast, his backward steps bringing him closer to the door, "I... I... went to Dahlem Evangelical Church... while... while Martin Niemöller was its pastor. My mother was—" But he choked; he could say no more.

Stumbling like a blind man, he left the house.

Borghild watched him go, watched the heavy plodding of his feet. She saw him turn and look back, as though he wanted to return... not to tell her of his love, but to ask her the way back to the ways he had once known. But he was bound by strong fetters.

And so he stumbled on.

Eighteen

IT WAS DARKER than the night of the invasion, and at sundown it had begun to rain. The somber clouds, clinging to the horizon at all of its contacts with the landscape, did sentry duty to the stars, and not one shaft of light broke through. A blind man could have found his way about the town as easily as one of the fabulous Cimmerians, who dwelt in perpetual darkness.

There was no lightning, no distant thunder. Only the drizzle of precipitation trickling through the darkness from sky to earth—through darkness so Stygian it seemed to have form, so pressing one wanted to beat it away with his arms.

No light... No wind... No thunder. Only the rain, the slow patter of the rain, tapping at every window, streaming from every roof.

Bruno Schreckenbach was out in the rain. Hans Laub had demanded that he inspect his sentries, for no one was to escape to the woods or the fjord through the opaque outskirts of the town. He had two armed men with him, and they avoided the streets.

"Why don't the people turn on the lights in their houses?" one of his accomplices asked. "It is early yet."

"Quiet!" Schreckenbach shouted in a whisper.

He did not need to explain himself to an inferior; he did not need to tell the two with him that he wanted them to be silent because he feared the darkness, and the treacheries it might hold for him, should any of the men know he was about.

At the town limits, he asked the first sentry, "Is all well?"

"Yes."

"You are sure no one will get by you in the darkness?"

The sentry assured, "There are dead branches all along the woods. If anyone tried to escape, we would hear the twigs snap, and then we would turn on the lights and—"

"But this rain," Schreckenbach warned. "It muffles the sound."

"Our ears are alert."

"If anyone escaped, Hans Laub would—" A twig snapped. "Turn on your light! Someone is trying to escape!"

The sentry flashed his piercing spotlight into the direction of the sound. The eyes of a dog glared back. Perhaps it was the same dog that had frightened Schreckenbach before.

"Get home, hound!" Schreckenbach cursed, throwing a heavy stick at the fleeing dog. He sighed, "No one must escape! No one!"

"No one will. I assure you."

One by one, he visited his sentries, warned them, admonished them. Some of them assured him with such confidence that he swore at them for being too casual.

He walked along the fjord—the sound of the drops against the water alluded to the slow strokes of a swimmer, and he compelled the water-front sentries to search the water with their lights. He walked past the ruined submarine base. He cursed when he walked over a concrete slab which the fjord had vomited onto the bank. One of the sentries stood near the battered hull of a U-boat burrowed into the sand.

"What will we do with the metal?" the sentry asked. "Salvage it?"

"Tonight," Schreckenbach snapped, "we will guard the town limits with our lives!"

"Yes, Herr Schreckenbach."

And he walked on.

The inspection orbit ended on a lofty point above the town. His eyes were well accustomed-to the dark now, and as he looked down, he could see the outlines of the houses, and the occasional shimmer of light behind a drawn shade; it was like being in a psychic world, whose houses had form without substance.

He half expected ghostly forms to emerge from the dwellings— women and children with luminous blood streaming from machine—gun bullet wounds, young men demanding him to pay for the crime of having them shot for transgressing the limits of their own town, men compelling him to loose the knots about their necks.

He paced to the shelter of the nearest birch, cursing.

"What do you see, Herr Schreckenbach?" the sentry asked.

"Nothing!" he snapped, and then goose-stepped away —glad that the darkness had one virtue—it hid the blush upon his face.

But as he neared the first houses, his goose-stepping mellowed to catlike steps. He was glad when he reached the hotel.

Leif Hunseid and Hans Laub eagerly awaited him.

"Is all well?" Laub demanded.

"Yes."

"You are sure?"

"The sentries are confident."

"Did you tell them that any sentry who permitted anyone to break through his territory would be shot?"

"You didn't tell me to say that, Hans."

Laub muttered something inaudible.

"Don't be so worried, Hans," Leif Hunseid cheered. "Everything is going—"

Hans Laub drew his curse from the plummet-point. of profanity. "Can't you get it into your thick head how serious things are, Hunseid? You've got enough German blood in your veins to have a little sense!"

"But I still think," Bruno Schreckenbach said, "that you're jumping at con—"

"Shut up, Bruno! Shut up! Do you know What happens to Nazi fliers who drop their bombs in the English Channel and report direct hits, so they don't need to face the spitfires... when Goering finds out about their cowardice? Do yOu know—?"

"I tell you," Leif Hunseid interrupted, "that—"

"Shut up!" Of Schreckenbach he asked, "When are you taking the twenty-four hostages?"

"Do—?"

"Might be all right to throw in a few women this time. Maybe it would help—"

"Hans, do... do... do you—?"

"Schreckenbach! Are you turning yellow?"

"N-No ..."

"Why do you look at me, then, like you were scared to death?"

"I... I..."

Laub continued, "Why not take the hostages tonight?"

"The houses are dark."

"Dark? What do you mean?"

"The lights are out. Look through the window."

Hans Laub looked through the window, and looking, he cursed, "I would give an arm to know who did it? I would give both arms if the British had never bombed us! Hunseid, why didn't you find out from the people, so we could have had German planes here to surprise the R. A. F.? Why didn't you find—?"

"I never heard so much as a rumor, Hans! You know that! And I've been doing my best to find out who did it, but no one seems to know."

Laub asked, "Do you think you are suspected?"

"Ho!" Hunseid boasted. "Suspected? I suspected? They don't —"

"Don't be so proud of yourself! Shall I remind you again that we've made a," he swore, "failure of our years of planning here?" Leif Hunseid did not answer. Hans Laub continued his gaze at the window. "Why are there no more lights? Do," Hunseid and Schreckenbach thought they saw a twitch of fear in Laub's fearless eyes, "you suppose trouble is brewing? Do you think there will be an attempt to break through the sentries with the guilty one?" Now they knew they saw fear in his eyes! "Do you think they might storm the. hotel? Are the guards alert?"

"Yes, Hans," Schreckenbach assured. "Adolf sits with a machine gun at the door."

"Good!" Laub seemed to breathe a bit easier. "Hadn't you better round up hostages?"

"But the houses are—"

"Ring! Demand entrance in the name of the Gestapo!"

"If no one comes—"

"Break down the doors!"

"But—"

"Bruno!" Laub bellowed. "Are you trying to avoid taking the hostages? Are you—?"

"Shouldn't we give the people time? Shouldn't we—?"

"Time! Time! We haven't enough for ourselves! Go out and take the first twenty-four adults you find, men or women!"

"It would be easier tomorrow, Hans. There is less chance of revolt in the daytime."

"You'll take them in the morning?"

"Before noon. Or perhaps, if they go to church, when they return."

Laub grunted before he said, "All right. Well, if you haven't anything more, go. I've got to think! Can't expect you two to give me any solutions!"

And so Bruno Schreckenbach and Hans Laub left for their rooms.

Whatever fright Schreckenbach had known before was incomparable to his fears this night. He feared the blackness, feared lest a hand reach for his throat, feared that hidden eyes might be aiming at his heart.

He retired. But there was no sleep.

He thought of Borghild Gran. Did he love her? Could he know love, he who was a murderer? Could a man be the agent of hate and the seeker of love simultaneously? And if he did gain her for the spoils, what then?

He tossed restlessly...

His thoughts remained in the Gran family. He thought of the minister. In the seclusion of his soul, where reason could exist unadulterated, he knew Prest Gran's way of life was right. He knew this man was a saint... and that he was a sinner. He knew Prest Gran faced a blessed eternity, that that was why the minister took things as he did... and that he was destined to an opposite eternity;

that that was why his thoughts frothed against his stained heart. He thought of Prest Gran's sermons, of his personal admonitions, of the challenge of his life.

And then he thought of Borghild Gran once more. Was he brute enough to kill the man she loved? Could he crush her heart so that, incapable of ever loving again, she would be his puppet?

Time idled along. These thoughts marched through his brain, over and over again. He could not sleep. He could only stare, Wide-eyed, into the darkness, while the weird rain played discordant accompaniment to the chantings in his head.

Would morning never come? Was this eternity? Was he dead, awaiting the justice of which he had been warned?

He stood and shook himself until convinced of reality.

And then he returned to his bed. But he did not sleep. He wondered if he would ever sleep again.

The silence! The darkness! The rain! His thoughts! They were driving him mad! He got up and turned on his light.

Yet, though now it was light, it was too dark for him to sleep.

Nineteen

BY DAYBREAK the rain subsided, at dawn the clouds parted, and at sunup the skies were clear.

Borghild had had a few hours of sleep. But it was not dreamless. And the dreams were not pleasant. Nor were the hours she lay awake pleasant, for they were filled with her perplexity. Was she a traitor? How could she be? Should she confess? How could she face brutal Hans Laub as the one Who had ruined his plans? And if she did not confess...

"Will the hostages be taken today," Bjarne asked at breakfast, "on the Lord's Day?"

Borghild trembled—for she had not told Bjarne that he was to be one of those who would die... if she did not confess.

Prest Gran said, "The Lord's Day means nothing to the Nazis. They wouldn't hesitate to commit their vilest brutalities on Sunday!"

Borghild's trembling renewed its intensity. Beneath the table cloth, she clutched her hands.

Sigurd scoffed, "It was on Friday morning, last September first, that German troops crossed the borders of Poland, but it was Sunday when Hitler's ultimatums to Chamberlain and Daladier expired and war was declared! Sunday's no different than any other day to them!"

"I have a funeral for twelve tomorrow," Prest Gran sighed. "I hope never to have a mass funeral again!"

"Oh!" Borghild shrieked.

"Borghild!" her father exclaimed. "What's the matter?"

"I... I... Oh, it's so horrible!" She stood, tottering. "I can't eat," she said, beginning to weep. "Please excuse me."

"I'm sorry, dear. Please eat with us. We won't talk about unpleasant things."

"No, thank you, Father. I... I'm not hungry... not at all... I... I'd rather go to my room... please."

Bjarne comforted, "Don't worry, sweetheart. Everything will be all right! I know it will!"

His words drew her eyes to him, made her stare at him... and wonder if he would be that optimistic if he knew.

"All things work together for good," her father quoted, "to them that love God. After we've been in heaven for a hundred years," he smiled faintly, "we will have forgotten all our earthly cares... perhaps," he said slowly, "even the way in which we died."

"Father!"

"Borghild," Bjarne urged, "please don't be so excited. Everything is going to be all right. God hasn't forsaken us."

"I'm sorry. I'll go to my room."

"Forgive me, dear," her father pleaded, "if I frightened you."

"You needn't apologize, Father." She made a brave attempt to smile, but' it was only an attempt. "I'll be ready in time for church."

She left and went to her room.

"Poor girl," Prest Gran moaned. "This is no place for women. I wish a break would come, so the women could get away from here."

"Do you think things will break?" Bjarne asked.

"Something is going to happen, I'm sure. Everything has its boiling point."

Sigurd said, "And if we do have to stay here, we at least have the peace of knowing that the submarine base has been destroyed."

"Yes," his employer said, "I'm sure all who have paid with their lives... or who may have to pay with their lives, feel it was worth the price. It nearly killed me, knowing the Nazis were using Bjerkely as a base for their destructions. I haven't that burden now, anyway."

"But who," Bjarne puzzled, "ever got the information to the British? And how?"

"We may never know, Bjarne."

Sigurd growled, "I wish I had done it, so I could have the fun of telling Laub and Schreckenbach how I fooled them!"

"The censorship is airtight. No one has escaped from the town." Bjarne thought a moment. "Do you think some of the men might have rowed out in boats and met the British somewhere... but that's far fetched, isn't it?"

"It's one of the most mysterious things I've known," Prest Gran said.

They talked on in this fashion, until breakfast was consumed.

In her room, Borghild had finished praying. Now she was thinking, trying to make plans. Perhaps she should go to Leif Hunseid's hotel and reveal her identity as the one who had betrayed the Nazis. Schreckenbach would mediate. Then, with the confession made, there would be no more reprisals. And what would happen to her? Would Schreckenbach, angered at her attitudes toward him, refuse to plead mercy for her? They might hang her in the town square, burn her at the stake... or send her to Berlin, to meet the fate of Polish and Jewish girls.

She prayed again. "Heavenly Father, I'm absolutely depending upon Thee for guidance. I'm so weak in myself, Lord. I'm so afraid. But Thou art my strength, Father! Help me to relax upon Thy promises, Lord. Help me to know that all things do work together for good to them that love Thee! Please, Heavenly Father, please! In Jesus' Name... amen!"

Above the din of conflict, she had peace.

Her father, Bjarne and she went early to church. But when they arrived, the auditorium was nearly filled.

"Dear people!" Prest Gran thrilled. "These trials have been good for their faith. And," his thrill changed to ecstasy, "many have been born again, because of these dark days! If only one had seen his need of Christ, it has been worth the burden!"

"Whatever the price," Bjarne whispered, "it has been well worth the spiritual growth in my life!"

Whatever the price! Borghild suppressed an exclamation.

The organist began to play. Prest Gran left them. They entered.

When Prest Gran walked to the pulpit stairs, all could see the stain of blood upon his robe. They had seen it each Sabbath, since that day of slaughter. No one mentioned it to him. He spoke of it to no one. It bore silent testimony of his sorrow... and of his joy.

The people had never sung as they did today. There was not the shout of the suppressed in their music, but the tone of triumph. The organ faded away, when they praised forth a fortissimo of faith; its predominant volume was unheard when the hymns were concluded, and the muted melody of the final amens could as well have been sung *a cappella*.

When the time came for the sermon, all was silent.

Prest Gran bowed his head, and all heads bowed.

"Almighty God... whose ways are only just... whose promises are sure... be present with us now. Let Thy Holy Spirit come upon us with comforting and convicting power. May each of us realize that, with things as they are, this may be his last Sabbath. Let us heed Thy Word, search our hearts, and utter our prayers with the constant remembrance of the brevity of life. We need to see only in terms of eternity these days. Give us eyes to see how true that is... In Jesus' Name... amen."

Borghild steadied herself. She tried to give full attention to the sermon. But she was thinking... of the brevity of life... and it was not easy to listen.

But, as her father's voice increased its volume, she gave ear.

Prest Gran, having seen that there were no uniforms in the audience, digressed from his notes. "My dear people, these are dark days, and yet they are bright days. Gloom need not cast its shadows across the Christian life! We have seen our prayers answered! And more of our prayers shall be answered, until the day Norway emerges free again!"

Borghild listened eagerly.

"I begged you to be patient, only that we might await the opportunity to strike. I didn't know what that opportunity would be, nor when it would come. But it came. And perhaps one of you in the audience had the great privilege of doing a historic service to your country. I am proud of you, whoever you are! I am proud that Bjerkely had one with the ingenuity to do such a service! I haven't been outspoken against Nazism, for its evils needed no elaboration! But I hate it, with the anger which is not sin! And I am more than willing to pay with my life, if necessary, now that our hope has been realized, and the submarine base destroyed!"

Borghild saw that her father's enthusiasm was reflected on the faces about her. Reflected? No, it emanated from the faces about her! They were proud! They were glad she had done it! And they would be glad to die, if necessary! She was happy. The tears deluged her eyes. She was happy!

"Heil Hitler!" thundered from behind the last pew.

All faces turned toward the door.

Hans Laub, Bruno Schreckenbach, and two officers of the Gestapo gooSe-stepped to the front of the auditorium.

Laub bellowed, "Religious idiots! I have a score to settle with you, and it's going to be settled if everyone of you has to die, so I can be sure the traitor has paid with his life!"

Prest Gran couldn't move his lips, nor did he move.

"Herr Schreckenbach!" Laub continued. "Select twenty-four men and women to die in the church yard, unless the traitor confesses!"

Borghild wanted to speak, but her lips seemed paralyzed. She watched, horror stricken, as Bruno Schreckenbach pointed to men and women in the pews, commanding them to stand to their feet and step to the aisle.

And then, Bruno Schreckenbach cried, but not without a distinct tremor in his voice, "Bjarne Kolstad! Step to the aisle!"

Borghild saw Bjarne stand beside her, move slowly to the aisle. Arrows of fear shot through her. She wanted to cry out. But she could not. Yet she had to! She had to!

Desperately, she stood, shouting, "Don't call any more names! I am the guilty one! I sent the information to the British!"

"Miss Gran!" Schreckenbach exclaimed.

"Borghild!" Bjarne gasped. "What are you saying?"

Hans Laub, a portrait of amazement, was silent.

"It's true! I sent a letter to my cousin in Stockholm!" She was brave. Her voice was firm. There were no tears. "I put a commemorative stamp from my brother's collection on the envelope, because my cousin is a stamp collector! Underneath the stamp, I wrote a message! I knew she would soak the stamp from the envelope paper in water, so the message would be read! I told her the British had to bomb Bjerkely's water front! I told her! I'm glad I did! Hans Laub! Bruno Schreckenbach! Do you hear me? I'm glad I did!"

Hans Laub's profanity exceeded any previous utterance. It was ten seconds before he demanded, "Take her out to be shot, Bruno!"

"No!" Schreckenbach shouted.

"No? Do you hear me? Take her out to be shot!"

Bjarne pleaded, "Don't shoot her! Let me die in her place!"

"Take him, too, Bruno!" Laub cursed.

Prest Gran came running from the platform. "No! No! Spare them! They are young! Take me! I am old! Take me!"

"Take the three of them, Bruno!" Laub sneered. "Chances are they conspired!"

Bruno Schreckenbach's eyes met Borghild's. He found them defiant. And in them he saw that she would never be his. It angered him. He would make her pay for her stubbornness! If he could not have her, no one else would!

"You three!" he ordered. "March to the church yard!" And to the people, restless in their pews, "Sit still, until we have gone outside! Then you may watch! Remember, we have guns!"

"Oh, Bjarne!" Borghild whispered, clutching Bjarne's arm.

"Brave, honey! We'll go together! We'll see your mother... Lars!"

"Father!" She gave her other arm to Prest Gran. "Did I do wrong?"

"No, my dear! I am proud of you! But," he choked, "I don't want to see you die!" To Schreckenbach, he pleaded, "Spare them, Mr. Schreckenbach! Take me, but—"

"Get outside, the three of you!"

They marched outside.

The shadows of the church spire, and its cross, lay upon the church yard. Birds were singing. The sun was radiant. A gentle breeze came from the fjord.

The people filed out of the church like wax figures, for their features were frozen in the icy clutches of horror.

"Stand over there!" Schreckenbach demanded, pointing to the fence.

"Please!" Prest Gran pleaded. "Let me die, but spare them! They are—"

"If you are so anxious, you go first!" Schreckenbach shouted. "Then it won't bother you... whatever we do to them!"

Bravely, Prest Gran stepped to the fence.

"Father! Father!" Borghild cried.

"Be brave, dear! Be brave!" he called to her.

Bjarne held her in his arms.

The anticipated radiance of heaven came to Prest Gran's face. He said, "For to me to live is Christ, and to die is gain. Blessed Christ! Soon I shall see Thee... face to face! Yea, he is altogether lovely!"

The two Gestapo officers had taken their places, lifted their guns. They were awaiting Schreckenbach's orders to fire.

But Schreckenbach could not give those orders. His bravery had been short-lived. He was remembering the Prest's sermons. He thought of his sleepless night, of the deaths he had already caused. And here was the greatest saint in Bjerkely... the greatest, perhaps, in all Norway.

"Why do you hesitate, Mr. Schreckenbach?" Prest Gran asked. "I am ready to go! I am eager! Why do you hesitate?" He looked heavenward, "In my Father's house are many mansions: if it were not so, I would have told you. I go—"

"Be quiet!" Schreckenbach screamed.

Laub cursed. "Give firing orders, Bruno! What are you waiting for?"

"I...I..."

"Please, Mr. Schreckenbach!" Prest Gran urged. "I am eager to meet my God! My wife is waiting to see me... and my son!"

Schreckenbach's eyes rolled like the eyes of a mad man, and he made three attempts before he commanded his men, "Load! Aim!" But then his tongue knotted, for Prest Gran was singing:

> In the sweet by and by,
> We shall meet on that beautiful shore;
> In the sweet by and by,
> We shall meet on that beautiful shore.

"Bruno!" Hans Laub cursed again. "Why don't you finish?"

Schreckenbach's chest surged as he filled his' lungs. Then he shouted, as he turned his face, "Fire!"

The rifles cracked.

"Father!" Borghild fell, limp, into Bjarne's arms.

Prest Gran's first expression, when the guns found their mark, was a smile. And then his face contorted in pain, as he collapsed.

His lifeless form fell across the shadow of the cross. A stream of blood issued from his body, covering the stain left by the blood of his son, and pouring out upon the ground... upon the shadow of the cross! He was spilling his blood upon the shadow of the cross, just as the Saviour he loved had given His on the Cross of Calvary!

It was pathetic and beautiful.

Bruno Schreckenbach's face was pale, when he turned to see what he had done. A violent sense of his guilt came over him. He had killed Prest Gran, the man, who, in spite of the ill the Nazis had done, had offered to show Bruno Schreckenbach the Way to the Land he had now entered.

"Bruno!" Hans Laub reminded. "There are two more!"

He had killed Prest Gran! He had killed Prest Gran! That was all he could hold in his mind.

"Bruno! There are two more! ...Bruno!" Laub cursed. "You!" he shouted at Bjarne and Borghild, who now stood. "Get up there beside the minister!"

With his arm about her waist, Bjarne led the woman he loved to the arm of the cross-shadow that protruded to the left of Prest Gran's body.

"Bruno!" Hans Laub demanded. "Kill these two! Bruno!"

Schreckenbach turned to Bjarne and Borghild. Borghild Gran! The woman he wanted... but could not have! He was to kill her... and the man she loved!

"Load!" he called to his men.

"Bjarne dear! Hold me tightly!"

"Sweetheart!"

"Aim!" Schreckenbach's voice rang out.

Borghild's beauty was its best, under the noonday sun. Her hair, gently yielding to the persuasions of the breeze, glowed like strands of fine gold. Her eyes were clear, forward-looking, as though they saw beyond the horizon, following the footsteps of her father's soul. Her lovely face... her tender lips...

"No!" Schreckenbach yelled. "I can't murder them! I can't! No! I can't!"

Laub burst, "Bruno, you fool! Order your men to shoot, or I will!"

"No! I can't! I can't!"

"Idiot!" Hans Laub cursed. "You!" he called to the Gestapo officers. "Are your guns loaded? Aim!"

The Gestapo officers aimed their rifles. The one on the right, for so they had planned between themselves, aimed at Borghild's heart. The one on the left aimed at Bjarne's heart.

"Fire!" was on Hans Laub's lips, when the roar of a motor captured his attention.

An armored car approached the crowd of people.

The Gestapo officers, trained rigidly only to obey orders, lowered their guns.

"Bruno!" Hans Laub gasped. "It's the commander of our Nazi forces... from Oslo."

The commander, a huge German with all the Nazi hardness of Hans Laub, and more, upon his face, leaped from the car.

"Laub!" he shouted. "The men at the hotel said we'd find you here!" Prest Gran's body took Only a moment of his attention. He was accustomed to sights like that. "Is it true that you let information slip by you, so the R. A. F. bombed our base here?"

"I... I..." Laub whined like a frightened child. "We've found the guilty one, and—"

"You mean I've found the guilty ones! Swine! You and Schreckenbach get into the car! You, too, Hunseid!

"You're going to answer in the presence of the Führer for this!"

"But—"

"You and Schreckenbach! Get in the car!"

"We—"

The Nazi commanded his aides, "Handcuff them, men!"

There was much confusion. The sentries, recognizing the military car, obeyed the impulses of their curiosity. There was no one watching the town limits, which touched the woods. And it was not far to the woods. Suddenly, there was the beating of feet, like many horses galloping.

"To the woods!" a man shouted. "To the woods!"

Hardly knowing what he was dOing, Bjarne took Borghild's hand and followed.

Not a shot was fired. The Nazis were utterly confused by the swiftness of the free men as they leaped from their cages.

Those who stayed behind saw Bruno Schreckenbach and Hans Laub handcuffed and led, like dogs, to the commanding officer's armored car. That pleased them. But when they saw their mayor, Leif Hunseid, handcuffed and taken with Schreckenbach and Laub, they were surprised. And then, after the car had driven away bearing its captives to Oslo, they began to talk, to offer suggestions as to why Leif Hunseid had been taken. There could be but one reason... Leif Hunseid was a Quislinger, a traitor to the people of Bjerkely!

Twenty

BJARNE AND BORGHILD lost the others in the woods. They ran until they came to a stream—a stream which fed its water to the fjord, a stream along whose banks they had often strolled. Exhausted, they stopped.

"Bjarne!" she began to cry. "Father is..."

"Your father is very happy, dear," he comforted. "He is with the Lord. And we have been spared!"

"He is happy," she said, forbidding the tears. "Father is happy." Then the tears came again, as she cried, "He was such a wonderful man, Bjarne! He was so kind... so Christlike... so wonderful! My dear father! He's dead, Bjarne! He's .dead! My father is dead! The Nazis killed him, Bjarne! They killed him!"

"The Nazis killed him," Bjarne said, stroking the back of her head, "but the angels of God took him Home!"

"Thank you, Bjarne!" she smiled. "Thank you for saying that!"

"It's true!"

"Yes... so very true!"

He kissed her.

"Will the Nazis leave now?" she asked.

"I don't know, dear. At least Hans Laub and Bruno Schreckenbach must leave."

"Bruno Schreckenbach!" she gasped.

"He was a brute, wasn't he?"

"Oh, Bjarne! You... You don't know!"

"Don't know? What don't I know?"

"He... He made... love to me."

"Schreckenbach?"

"Yes. Oh, it was horrible!"

"But—"

"He would come, when I was home alone, and... and sometimes I met him in the cemetery."

Bjarne's eyes strained at their sockets.

"I didn't let him love me, Bjarne. I couldn't. He's so horrible! But I had to get that letter mailed, and—"

"Didn't you send the letter at the post office?"

"No. I sent the letter before postal service was restored. I sent it with Bruno Schreckenbach. Oh, Bjarne, can you ever forgive me?"

"Forgive you! I'm proud of you!"

"Thank you, Bjarne!" She drew his lips to hers. "I will always be true to you... always!"

"Sweetheart!"

There were no words for a minute.

"Bjarne, was it worth it?"

"You mean...?"

"So many lives were lost. Father..." She choked. "Oh, Bjarne, should I have done what I did? Twelve were killed! And... and then Father! Did I do right?" she sobbed.

"Listen to me, darling. Please don't cry for a moment."

She looked up at him.

"Borghild," he grasped her chin with his right hand, supported her head with his left hand, "our way of reasoning has not been trained to see the cruel things of war. But there are times when death is triumph. Thank God, each of those who died has gone to be with the Lord!" He smiled, as he asked, "Do you think any of them would want to return?"

"But... the widows... the fatherless children... the—"

"They will praise your heroic work as long as they live, sweetheart! Remember, it was Schreckenbach and Laub, not you, who put the men to death! You did what all of us wanted to do! You need have no regrets!"

"Thank you, Bjarne! I'll try to see it that way!"

"Dear girl! My heroine!"

They kissed again.

A throat was cleared behind them.

"Sigurd!" Borghild exclaimed.

"I found you," he smiled. "Come with me."

"Where to, Sigurd?" Bjarne asked.

"About ten of us single men escaped to the woods," he informed. "We're going to travel by night to the Swedish border, so we can get to England on a Swedish boat and join the Allies in one way or another."

"Good idea! Let's join them, Borghild!"

"B-But," she struggled once more with tears, "m-my father. He hasn't been buried."

"I... I," Sigurd's lips wavered, "loved him!"

Sigurd wept bitterly.

Borghild placed her arm on his shoulder. "We'll see him some day, Sigurd!"

"We will!" he sobbed. "We'll see him in heaven some day... by the grace of God!"

"Bjarne, we've got to go back to Bjerkely and bury my father."

"As you say, dear."

Sigurd hesitated, "But... But... don't you want to go with us to Sweden?"

"Yes," Borghild said, "only—"

"If I know the people of Bjerkely," Sigurd swallowed the lurking sobs, "they'll tenderly lay Prest Gran's body in a grave beside his wife. There's nothing more we could do. I... I wouldn't be bossy, but... but if you were to ask me, I'd tell you that it's my opinion your father would want you to go with us, Borghild, so we can have a real part in helping the Allies make Norway free again."

"I... I think he's right, Bjarne."

"I do too."

"Father is gone. It would only hurt all the more to see his corpse." She whispered bravely, "We will go... to Sweden... to England... for the liberation of Norway!"

"Good!" Sigurd beamed. "Come with me! It won't take our party long to get to Sweden! Thank God! We can do something now—something for Norway... and Bjerkely!"

"Goodbye, Bjerkely," Borghild whispered, as she . and Bjarne followed Sigurd, "we may not see you for many months, but we'll be back... after we have helped to make you free. Goodbye, Bjerkely!"

"Goodbye, Bjerkely," Bjarne repeated.

The End

Printed in the United States of America

How Can You Find Peace With God?

The most important thing to grasp is that no one is made right with God by the good things he or she might do. Justification is by faith only, and that faith resting on what Jesus Christ did. It is by believing and trusting in His one-time *substitutionary* death for your sins.

Read your Bible steadily. God works His power in human beings through His Word. Where the Word is, God the Holy Spirit is always present.

Suggested Reading: New Testament Conversions by Pastor George Gerberding

Benediction

Now unto him that is able to keep you from falling, and to present you faultless before the presence of his glory with exceeding joy, To the only wise God our Savior, be glory and majesty, dominion and power, both now and ever. Amen. (Jude 1:24-25)

More Than 100 Good Christian Books For You To Download And Enjoy

The Book of Concord. Edited by Henry Eyster Jacobs and Charles Krauth.

Henry Eyster Jacobs. *Summary of the Christian Faith*

Theodore Schmauk. *The Confessional Principle and The Confessions of The Lutheran Church As Embodying The Evangelical Confession of The Christian Church*

George Gerberding. *Life and Letters of William Passavant*

Joseph Stump. *Life of Philip Melanchthon*

John Morris. *Life Reminiscences of An Old Lutheran Minister*

Matthias Loy. *The Doctrine of Justification*

Matthias Loy. *The Story of My Life*

William Dau. *Luther Examined and Reexamined*

Simon Peter Long. *The Great Gospel*

George Schodde *et al. Walther and the Predestination Controversy. The Error of Modern Missouri*

John Sander. *Devotional Readings from Luther's Works*

A full catalog of all 100+ downloadable titles is available at LutheranLibrary.org .

Printed in Great Britain
by Amazon

80194970R00128